# THE BILLIONAIRE'S FORTUNATE ACCIDENT

*A Doctor Romance (Irresistible Brothers Book 8)*

## SCARLETT KING

## MICHELLE LOVE

# CONTENTS

Published in the USA by Scarlett King & Michelle Love

©Copyright 2021

ISBN-13: 978-1-63970-038-7

 Created with Vellum

# BLURB

**I'm single, charming, and a billionaire!**
**I've got everything a man could want.**
**Except someone to truly love...**

As a trained chef, I was expected to open a restaurant within
the resort that my brothers and I owned.
But I still hadn't found the type of food I wanted to serve to
our esteemed guests.
Something was missing deep in my soul.
I would've never thought that one drunken night of partying
could lead to finding the love of my life.
Even a fast-food uniform couldn't dull her natural beauty —
inside and out.
I'd dreamt of her that night, and it had been beautiful.
She's so much more than she appears to be.

**This perfect woman is going to be a doctor.**

# CHAPTER 1

# STONE

The powerful beat of Lil Jon and DJ Snake's "Turn Down for What" moved through the nightclub like an invisible wave on an ever-moving ocean. And there I was, right in the middle of it all, fists pounding the air above my head, shoulders bumping against those of my buddies, mouth wide open and shouting the words along with the tracks the DJ was playing for us.

*Not a care in the world.*

I'd just turned twenty-seven. The number sounded magical to me. No longer a young man in his early twenties, I was now considered to be in my mid- to late-twenties. Somehow, that just sounded cooler to me, more mature.

But this was no typical birthday for me. The day had started with me spending time at the resort my older brothers and I owned in Austin, Texas. I'd been pampered by the spa staff — a pedi and mani, of course, plus a deep tissue massage that left me feeling like I was lying on a bed made of clouds.

*A perfect way to start my birthday.*

Whispers Resort and Spa was the best thing that had ever happened to my brothers and me. It had opened up all five of our lives in ways we'd never expected. Only, my brother all had found their callings relatively easily, while I was still working on finding mine.

As a trained chef, my brother expected me to open a restaurant within the resort. But I still hadn't found the type of food I wanted to serve to our esteemed guests.

In my defense, coming up with a menu wasn't easy when we served food to such distinguished clientele. People came from around the world to check out the resort. Important people. Dignitaries, famous singers and musicians, actors and actresses, senators, congressmen, and even the president himself had visited our resort.

Anyone would've felt the pressure to be perfect — to serve only the most perfect food. We already had one restaurant, Essence, which had garnered a Micheline star. We'd also had one restaurant fail, while one other one was doing just okay.

I didn't want to fail or be just okay. I wanted to give Essence a run for its money. The only problem with doing something like that was that my brothers thought that might not be the best for business. So, I had to design a menu that did not have a single thing similar to anything on Essence's diverse menu.

*Complicated, I know.*

One of the guys in our group came bouncing in with another round of beers. "You got the next round, Stone."

Nodding, I took one of the beers and gulped down the first half. "You bet, Terry."

Mike looked in one direction as a group of ladies danced their way toward us. "Incoming. I got the redhead."

"I'll take any of the blondes," Terry informed us.

"Five of them, five of us," Monty added.

One of the lovely ladies had her dark eyes on me. Long, dark hair cascaded down to a teeny tiny waist. I was sure she must have had worn a waist-trainer for her to be that thin. Her v-neck cropped sweater made her huge breasts stand out. They were too full, too perfect, and that meant they were completely fake.

She wiggled her extremely round ass in front of me as if to entice me to grind on it, so I did as she expected, finding it as firm as concrete. *Geeze, this is fake, too!*

My generation — one of supreme fakery — wasn't to my liking. I'd take a natural waist, bust, and ass any day over a bunch of fake shit.

Turning her head, she looked back at me with the longest, lushest, darkest eyelashes that I'd ever seen. "You're good, boy."

A nod was the best I could do as I took her waist in my hands, pulling her closer to me. Grinding her fake ass harder, I felt the wet heat coming from underneath her extremely short skirt. Her six-inch heels compensated for her short stature, making her ass level with my groin area.

Again, I started thinking about my generation and the utter lack of any real dance moves. We jumped up and down. We simulated sex on the dancefloor. We even swayed back and forth in unison. But we never made any graceful moves. We never actually danced.

Maybe it was because it was my birthday and I'd become another year older — I didn't know for sure — but I wasn't feeling the same vibes I usually felt when I was out with my friends. I didn't usually fall into existential contemplation while dancing groin to ass with a complete stranger.

Whatever my problem was, I knew one sure way of curing it. "I'm going for another round." Letting go of the girl's waist, I left her ass swinging on its own — I don't think she even realized I'd walked away.

Moving through the thick crowd, I finally made it to one of the bars and found a free seat, a rare accomplishment. Taking it, I held up one finger to signal to the bartender.

Bouncing over to me, the sassy young woman asked, "What can I get ya, handsome?"

"Drunk," I let her know.

"Got ya." She turned around, grabbed a short glass then filled it up with various alcohols. Placing it in front of me, she said, "Texas Tea, sans ice. It's strong and dangerous. But I'm sure a man of your muscular stature can handle this little ol' drink."

I took it like it was a shot. "Another one, please."

"Holy shit!" She made me another one, but this time offered me some sage advice, "Don't drive home."

"I got here in an Uber, and I'll leave in one too." I drank this one a bit slower as I turned to scan the room. It was filled with people jumping up and down to the bouncy beat of the Jonas Brothers' song, "It's Only Human."

*It's only human, you know that it's real*
*So why would you fight or try to deny the way that you feel?*
*Oh, babe, you can't fool me, your body's got other plans*
*So stop pretending you're shy, just come on and*
*Dance, dance, dance, dance…*

Lost in the lyrics, I wondered if anyone was really shy anymore. No one in this club seemed shy in the least. I saw no wallflowers hanging out along the outer edges of the crowd.

*Early morning la-la-light*
*Only getting up to close the blinds, oh*
*I'm praying you don't change your mind*
*Cause leaving now just don't feel right*
*Let's do it one more time, oh babe…*

I had to wonder why there were so many songs about sex. This particular song was about sex with a stranger. Two people meet in a bar or a nightclub, just like this one, go home together, and get right down to the nitty-gritty. The dirty deed. The horizontal mambo. Whatever you wanted to call it, it was one thing, and that thing was human. Being human. Needing another human to make things seem as if they were okay.

Scratching that itch alone could be alright and was

4

certainly great for giving a person some relief. But having sex with a partner is a whole different story — a much better one. For a long time in my life, I hadn't even cared what partner I had — just as long as I had one.

Staring at all the jumping, humping strangers, it suddenly hit me that something had changed inside my brain with this birthday. There had to be more to life than just partying.

*What would that be? I don't know yet.*

My brothers had all found their soulmates and produced some offspring. While I enjoyed playing with my nieces and nephews, I hadn't really wanted one a kid of my own. And I hadn't wanted a woman of my own either.

I preferred playing the field. The bachelor lifestyle had suited me just fine. But as I looked around, I couldn't find a single woman who turned me on. Gyrating females usually did the trick for me, but not on this night.

Downing the remainder of my drink, I turned back to find the bartender shaking her head at me. "What's wrong?" she asked.

"I'm not sure. Something is, though. Maybe another one of these will help me understand better." I slid the empty glass across the bar.

Even though she took the glass to refill it, she wasn't going to do it without giving me her input first. "I've never seen a single incident where alcohol helped someone understand anything any better. But here you go anyway." She placed the drink in front of me. "If I start to see you wobbling on that barstool, I'm calling you a cab."

"You're a very mindful person." I took a sip of the drink, which burned as it went down my throat.

"I am that." She left me to tend to her other customers, probably offering them more of her wise words as well.

Terry's tall form emerged from the dancers, his eyes on me. "There you are. You've got this round, Stone."

"I forgot." Signaling the bartender, who only shook her head at me, I shrugged. "She's not gonna hurry to get me anything. This is my third Texas Tea."

"What's up, Stone?" Terry leaned on the bar between me and another guy who was sitting on the next stool. "Is turning twenty-seven getting to ya or what?"

"I don't know, man. Like, I really *don't* know. I'm just not feeling this right now. I'm trying to." I held up the drink. "Hence this strong concoction that I'm pouring down my gullet. But it hasn't changed anything thus far."

"Four beers," he shouted to the bartender and then looked back at me. "I'm thirty. I know the kinds of things that go through a man's head after getting to the end of their twenties. Things like, 'Will I be expected to settle down with some woman and end the best days of my life now?'"

"Well, is it expected of me?" I didn't want that at all.

"How should I know? All I do know is that it went through my mind. Other things did too. Such as having kids before it was too late."

"Men can have kids forever. I'm not even worried about that."

"Yeah, they can make babies forever, but you only have a set number of good years in you. You'll want to play with your kids, right? You'll want to live to see them graduate high school, college, and get married, and have kids of their own. You won't be able to do that if you don't have kids until you're old."

"Sounds like you've thought a lot about this. But I should point out that you're thirty and still single with no kids." I smiled. "That we know about, anyway."

"Hey," he said as he took the four beers into his hands. "I always wear a slicker in a rainstorm. So, don't even joke about me having a kid that I don't know about. That's like a nightmare to me."

Standing up to go back to the dancefloor with him, I felt slightly woozy and sat back down. "I think I'm gonna head home, Terry."

"K. I'll let the guys know. Happy birthday."

"Yeah." As I looked over my shoulder to signal to the bartender that I was ready to settle my tab, she stood there with her hand held out. I already knew what she wanted — I unlocked my cell and handed it to her. "The address is saved. But I want to get something to eat before I go home. Can you type in the address of a nearby burger joint?"

The next thing I knew, I was in the back of a small Toyota Camry pulling up at an all-night fast food dive called Hamburger Hut. "Thanks, man. You don't have to wait. I'll call another driver when I'm done here."

Heading inside, I found the place mostly empty. One old guy sat in a booth alone, talking to himself. A girl stood behind the counter, chewing gum and looking bored. "Welcome to Hamburger Hut, where the customer is number one and so are the burgers. What can I get you?"

"A cheeseburger, all the way with mustard, mayo, and ketchup." I needed to fill my belly with something substantial to help soak up all the alcohol I'd put in it. Otherwise, I'd wake up with a horrendous hangover.

"Would you like the meal?" she asked. The bored tone in her voice made me certain that she'd asked the question a zillion times before. "You can have medium fries, onion rings, cheese sticks, hash brown potatoes, waffle fries."

I had a sense that she would go on and on if I didn't pick something fast. "Fries. Large, not medium. And do you have milk?"

She reached under the counter and pulled out a little milk carton. "We have this one that we use for the kid's meals."

"Give me ten of those." I pulled out my wallet, digging through it to find some cash. Putting a twenty down on the

7

counter, I decided was feeling generous. "You can keep the change."

"Wow, thanks," she said with lackluster enthusiasm. "A whole two bucks. You're a real hero."

"And you're a ray of sunshine." I went to find a seat. Looking at the plethora of empty tables, I chose one by a window that looked out at the nearly empty street.

Hookers, pimps, and partygoers were the only ones still out after midnight. I looked at my phone and realized it was nearly two in the morning. That's when I noticed a text from my oldest brother, Baldwyn. He wanted to remind me of an early meeting we were having the next morning. *Fuck! This morning!*

I had a meeting at eight and it was almost two now. Only six hours before I had to be at the resort, and there I was, sitting and waiting on food.

I needed to get some sleep. Even if it was only for a few hours. As soon as the smarmy chick brought me the food, I began scarfing down the fries and the milk. Once I unwrapped the burger from the yellow paper, I removed the top part of the bun so I could add some salt and pepper from the tiny packets she'd left on the tray.

*What the fuck is this?*

"Hey," I shouted. "I need to see someone about this — right now. Where's your manager?"

As I looked up at the counter, my vision blurred from the many spirits I'd consumed, but I saw someone hurrying my way. "What's the problem, sir?" she asked with a worried tone to her sweet voice.

"A big fat roach is the problem." I pointed at the thing, smack dab in the center of the meat patty. "I didn't order one with the extra insect on it."

"Oh, my gosh!" She leaned in, quickly wrapping the paper around the burger to hide the creepy, crawly thing. "I am so sorry. I'll get you your money back. Order anything you want. It's on the house." She was wearing a nervous expression. Her cheeks were pink, her lips trembled — the lower one plumper than the one on top — and her green eyes were wide with worry. She ran one hand over her straight, ash blonde hair that hung all the way down her back.

"Nah, it's okay."

# CHAPTER 2
## JESSA

"No, really, I'll give you your money back. This isn't okay. I'm not sure how this happened, but I can promise you that I'll get to the bottom of it." My cheeks were hot with embarrassment as I took the roach-filled burger, dumping it into the trash. I went to the register and pulled out a twenty, then went back to the man who was gazing at me with glassy eyes.

He'd been drinking; that was more than obvious. And I was sure he needed something in his stomach. Not that he would want anything we had to give him.

*A roach in his burger? Really people?*

Were it not for Hamburger Hut's tuition reimbursement perk, I wouldn't have stepped foot inside the door of this establishment. But I needed what they had to give, so I'd taken the job as night manager and had worked there for the last couple of years.

I'd brought a sandwich from home that night, so I went to the office and pulled it out of the mini fridge. I also had a bag of potato chips in the desk drawer, so I got that too before going back out to find the man who was still all smiles as he looked at me with what I could only describe as adoring eyes.

The man was something. Tall, muscular, with chiseled

features, and the deepest, darkest blue eyes I'd ever seen. His thick dark lashes made those blue eyes pop even more. Not that I cared about how hot he was. I was too busy for that sort of thing anyway. "Here you go. I'm giving you my lunch. I brought it from home."

"No, you don't have to do that." He waved his hand as if shooing me away. But then he reached out, taking my wrist. "Do you think the milk is safe to drink?"

"I do think so, sir." I placed the food in front of him. "I noticed that you ordered your burger all the way." I unwrapped the sandwich. "You need to eat something. I made this myself, so I know there's no bugs in it. Just fresh turkey, Swiss cheese, lettuce, tomato, and mayo inside. I think you'll like it."

He huffed as he looked at the food in front of him. "You think I'm drunk, don't you?"

"I'm not thinking that at all." I was totally thinking that, but the poor guy had already been served a roach burger, so I wasn't going to add anything else to that horrible experience by calling him drunk. "I just think that you came in here to eat, so I'm giving you something to eat. That's all."

"You're not wrong." He picked up one half of the sandwich. "I *am* drunk. I turned twenty-seven today. Well, yesterday, since it's now past midnight. And I was out at the club, partying with my best buds, when it hit me that I wasn't having fun. Not really. And then I went and sat at the bar, and that's when I got drunk." He gestured to the chair across the table. "Sit. Have a tiny carton of milk." He pushed one toward me.

I wasn't about to say no, since there was still a chance that he might sue the restaurant chain for the roach incident. "Thank you, sir. I'd love to join you." I took the milk, opened it then grabbed a straw off the nearby condiment shelf. "I haven't had one of these little things since grade school. These are really for the kid's meals." I took a sip and didn't care for it at all. "I prefer chocolate milk, though."

"Too much sugar in that kind." He took a bite of the sandwich. "This is good."

"Thanks." It was the first decent food I'd had in my fridge in a long time. "I splurged and spent some money on healthy-ish foods this last week. One of the doctors at the hospital I intern at gave me a lottery ticket scratcher, and I won five hundred bucks. So, I bought a hundred bucks worth of groceries, filled my car up with gas, and got an oil change. The poor thing hadn't had one in over a year. I've just been topping off the oil when it started running low."

Even when he looked confused, he was still as cute as could be. "You intern at a hospital? And you work here too?"

"I do."

He eyed me as he finished off the first half of the sandwich, and then picked up the other. "I'm Stone Nash." He cocked one dark brow. "And you are?"

"Jessa." I smiled. "It's nice to meet you, Stone. That's a very... Well, um, that's a very strong name you have there."

"Yeah, my mom liked ostentatious names. I've got four older brothers too. Baldwyn. Patton. Warner. Cohen. See, ostentatious." He took another bite. "Is Jessa short for something?"

"My mother was partial to ostentatious names as well." I found that an interesting coincidence about us. "My full name is Carolina Jessamine Moxon."

"Wow." He chuckled then he went on, "That's a mouthful, isn't it? My middle name is average — Michael."

"Stone Michael Nash." I thought it sounded anything but average. "Sounds like the name of a movie star to me."

"Carolina Jessamine Moxon sounds like the name of a rich girl to me."

*Wow, he's good.*

Not that I was about to talk about where I came from —

or from *what* I came from. "One day, I do hope to make something out of myself. I'm in my third year at Dell Medical School. The rest of this year, and one more, then I'll become what I've dreamed of since I was just a little kid — a doctor."

"You got any brothers or sisters, Carolina Jessamine?"

"I've got one older sister. Her name is Carolina Lily."

"Both of you are named Carolina?" He shook his head. "That must have been confusing."

"Not really. She was called Lily, and I was called Jessa." Looking at my watch, I realized that time had rushed by as we'd sat there talking. "Let me call you a ride before I get back to work, Stone."

He pulled his cell phone from his pocket, unlocked it then slid it towards me. "The app has my home address in it already. I'd do it myself, but my vision is still a little blurry — too many Texas Teas. The sandwich is helping, though. And your conversation is too. You and I should go out sometime. Like tomorrow night?"

"That's more than nice of you, but I don't have time to date, Stone. I'm flattered, really. But I can't go anywhere but to work and school." I ordered a car to pick him up, then slid his phone back to him. "Thanks for asking, though."

"No." He shook his head as he opened the bag of chips. "There is no way you can just not have time for a date. That's inhumane. There has to be a few hours in your week where you just sit there by yourself, not doing anything at all. We can go out during that time. Night or day — I don't care which or what time. I just want to take you out somewhere and spend some time with you. I like you. I like how nice you are. And you're really, really pretty too, even with that boring tan uniform that doesn't fit anyone well. I mean, look at that girl up there at the counter. She's as shapeless as a sack of potatoes."

Tammy held up her middle finger. I put my face in my

hands, thoroughly embarrassed at the lack of control I had over my employees. "Sorry about her."

"No offense," he slurred as he called out to her. "Everyone looks like a sack of potatoes in those things." Then he looked back at me. "Well, except you. Somehow, you're managing to pull it off."

"Management can order their uniforms to fit them. I guess they want us to stand out a bit from the employees who work under us."

"Clever." He sat back, crossing his arms over his broad chest. "Come on, Jessa. One date. If you hate it, then I'll never bother you again."

I was sure that I'd love going out with a man like Stone Michael Nash. But I hadn't been lying — I really didn't have any time for such a thing. "Stone, it's not that I want to tell you no. It's not that I want to turn you down. But I've got a full plate. I'm really sorry — I truly am. Even if we went out on one date and we really hit it off, then what?"

"I don't know." He smiled, making my heart melt.

"What if we hit it off, and then you end up hating me because I don't have enough time for you?"

"What if we're really lucky and hit it off, end up getting married, have kids, and even get a dog? Just say yes, Jessa. Don't make me come back here every night until you finally say yes."

No matter how tempting it sounded to be able to look at this cutie every night, I couldn't let him derail my plans. No matter how hot he was.

I dreamed of her that night, and it had been beautiful. Still, I woke with a headache. A couple of aspirins helped with that problem before I walked into the meeting with our cousins, the Gentry brothers.

The Gentry brothers had given us the startup money to get Whispers Resort and Spa going. Since opening and prospering from the venture, we'd grown in size. Warner had added two sister destinations to our family of resorts in Ireland, where he, his wife, and children lived.

Each of us was supposed to do something to further the group's accomplishments as a whole. Everyone else had done their part. I was the only one who hadn't added a single thing to the list of milestones that seemed to be growing each year.

Tyrell, Jasper, and Cash — the Gentry brothers — had come from Carthage, Texas, to hold the meeting. All my brothers were there too. Even Warner had flown in from Ireland for the yearly meeting.

Baldwyn took charge as we all sat at a large round table. "This meeting will come to order now that we're all here."

Patton took the minutes as he sat to the right of Baldwyn. "I've got the attendance written down. Tyrell, will you begin?"

"I'd love to, Patton." Tyrell opened the folder in front of him. "We've expanded the ranch to include the sale of only organic fruits and vegetables, using heirloom seeds that are non-GMO certified. My wife, Ella, has helped on this project as well. Thus far, our reach is only as far as our own lone star state of Texas. But we've projected inventory and sales that are expected to increase with each passing year. We hope to sell nationally within five years and globally within ten."

I clapped along with everyone else at our cousin's major accomplishment. The men in my group seemed to have ideas exploding in their heads at all times. While it seemed that I couldn't come up with a single one, no matter how hard I tried.

I wrote down that my cousins' ranch would now be producing organic, heirloom, non-GMO fruits and vegetables — as a chef, I thought that information might come in handy to me someday.

Patton congratulated Tyrell, "Great job, man. Now we'll hear from Jasper."

"Yeah, I've got some big news." He wore a grin that revealed more than he'd said so far. "My wife, Tiffany, and I have overseen the production of bull sperm, and we're now selling it on the Australian market. They've been wary of bringing in American genetics to their Australian herds. But I talked one rancher into it, and the stout calves born from our bulls' sperm and their cows have proven profitable. We're selling to over a hundred Australian ranchers now, and that number is growing all the time."

Clapping along with everyone else, I wondered how he'd come up with that idea. But I didn't ask.

"Another great job by the Gentry brothers," Patton exclaimed. "How about you, Cash?"

"Well, mine's a little different. See, I've gone in another direction. My wife, Bobbi Jo, and I have gone into the whisky-making business. Whisper Distillery is just in the beginning stages, but we've already gotten a lot of press attention out of the Dallas area. And a few bars have already reached out, wanting exclusive rights to the spirits we'll be producing. By next year's meeting, I should have some amazing numbers for y'all."

Jotting that down, I figured that'd be helpful if I ever opened a restaurant. "So, would I be able to get you to make something exclusive for my place too?"

"You've got a restaurant now?" Cash asked with a wide grin on his face. "That's awesome, Stone. I can't wait to check that out. And of course, we can come up with anything you want, cousin. We can work together on the fine spirits you'd like to serve at your place. What's it called?"

Baldwyn cleared his throat, drawing the attention off me. "He hasn't opened anything yet, Cash. My guess is he's just *asking* about that for right now."

My face was hot with embarrassment as I looked down at my notebook without saying a word. There was a valid reason why I didn't often speak up during our meetings. I had nothing to offer, and everyone knew that.

Patton moved on quickly. "Baldwyn, what have you and Sloan been up to this past year?"

"My wife and I have made some great adjustments to the daycare at Whispers Resort. We've added some specialty classes for each age group. Now, our employees and our guests can leave their children in the care of our highly accomplished staff and feel great, knowing that their kids are not only being entertained but are actually learning things too."

*And my oldest brother has gone so far as to come up with an idea to make kids smarter. Great.*

"One of the selling points to our guests is that there will be Spanish classes, so their kids will learn another language. A pretty essential language for Texas. But our teachers won't be teaching traditional Spanish either. They'll be teaching the Tex-Mex that's spoken around here."

Another round of applause. I joined in, feeling pretty shitty about myself. I had nothing to say, once again. If I tried, I would only come up with some lame ideas that would earn me blank stares as they all sat in silence. And then we'd adjourn. Only then would I be set free of this embarrassment.

"My turn," Patton said as he looked at each one of us. "Alexa and I have come up with a theme and range of products for the major chain Rooms for You. As you all know, my wife is a massage therapist. She came up with the idea of being able to purchase the things one needs to have a great massage and spa experience right at their own home. From the massage bed to the plants, water features, and sound systems that bring the whole thing together, we've designed and produced everything you will need to entirely transform one room in your home into a place of complete relaxation."

I had a question about that. "Won't you need an actual person to do the massages, Patton?"

"No, you won't. We've designed a weighted blanket that has different settings, so you can get the type of massage you want. It's filled with tiny stainless-steel balls that move on miniature tracks. I have to hand it to Alexa, really, for coming up with the idea and creating a prototype that we were able to get a manufacturer to produce in large quantities for us."

"Sounds pretty cool," I had to admit. "I bet it's pricey, though."

Patton nodded. "Right now, it is. But, like everything else, with time, the price will come down as we find cheaper ways of building it. Our clientele generally has the money to buy things that help them relax, though."

Baldwyn asked, "Do you have an exclusive with the store Rooms for You?"

"No. They're just the only one who said they'd pick it up."

"Well then, I say you put some products in one of the available spaces here at the resort. Why not directly sell to our guests as well?"

I couldn't believe Baldwyn had had a genuinely great idea

as he just sat there, listening to what our other brother had come up with. I felt like a total idiot, sitting amongst such great minds.

Patton added something to his notes then looked at Warner. "Okay, Warner, your turn."

"Cruises." Warner held up a picture of a large yacht. "Whisper Cruises will take guests from America to Ireland where they will stay in any one of our three bed and breakfasts."

"I thought you only had two," I blurted out.

"We've just added a third one," Warner said with pride.

"So, you have two accomplishments this year." My chest caved in with how stupid I felt.

"Orla found an abandoned farm outside Dublin, which we bought. We built small cottages that reflect a much older version of how the Irish used to live. It's rustic living, but so far, the guests love it. So, we have the two castles, and now, the Irish farm. And with this yacht that can carry up to thirty guests at a time, we can bring more people to our part of the world — in style."

I was really out of my league here. And I was sure they all knew that as well. But no one had pointed it out yet, which I was thankful for.

"Way to go, Warner. You guys are rocking over there." Patton turned his attention to Cohen. "I know you've been busy with the kids now that Ember is pregnant with twins, but I bet you've got something for us."

With a shake of his head, Cohen had no idea how happy he'd just made me. "Not really, Patton. I've had my hands so full that I've had just enough time to manage my duties here at the resort. But since the doctor ordered Ember to bedrest, and she's been stuck on her back all the time, she came up with this amazing idea. A baby hammock. It's a tiny hammock, just like a full-size one. You can hang it from hooks that you screw into either side of any wooden doorframe. Plus, there's a small battery pack that moves a mechanic arm back and forth to gently rock the baby. You can take this anywhere, and it's so compact that you can simply stash it inside any typical diaper bag. It's like having a rocker always at your fingertips."

*Holy shit! I'm going to be the only one without a single fucking idea of any kind.*

The dreaded moment came when there was no one left to speak but me. Patton smiled as he said, "Brilliant, Cohen. Your wife is one smart woman. Now onto you, Stone."

All eyes on me, I began to sweat. "Well, first, I'd like to congratulate you all on your major accomplishments this year. I come from good stock. So it seems." I chuckled, even though no one else did.

Tyrell raised one brow as he asked, "Have you come up with anything you'd like to cook and sell here at the resort? I know you don't have a whole menu yet, but you could start with one simple or not so simple food that you could sell right here. You know, like the way Cinnabon sells the one item. Or Chic-Filet sells their thing. You could begin with one thing. And I'm sure you could build a menu around it in no time at all."

"One thing, huh?" I didn't know what that one thing would be.

"And give yourself a timeline, Stone," Jasper added. "Say, a year, to get this one thing going."

Cash went on, "I'm sure you can find a little area at the resort where you can set up a few small tables and chairs to let the guests sit down and enjoy your food. It's a start, right?"

"The gift shop has free room," Baldwyn was quick to offer.

I wasn't about to open some little piece of crap inside the gift shop. "I don't think so."

"You don't think so about what?" Patton asked. "The whole idea? Or just the gift shop?"

"Kind of the whole idea." I was met with blank stares. "I

mean, it is a good idea, Tyrell. Don't get me wrong. But I have something a little different in mind."

"Great!" Tyrell shouted as he clapped his hands loudly. "You've got an idea then. Tell it to us. Give us some insight into what you want to do, Stone."

Warner looked at me with knowing eyes. "He doesn't have it mapped out yet."

"Not yet," I agreed.

Cohen chewed his lower lip then said, "One year, Stone. Give yourself just one year to come up with something that you can add to our group. We're not here to squash anyone's dreams. We're all here to help lift each other up. Feel free to talk to any of us about anything that comes to mind. No idea is too stupid to run by one of us, at least."

Nodding, I knew my time had come. *One year — time to stop messing around and get shit done.*

Sitting at the small desk in the back of Hamburger Hut, I heard a man asking, "Is Jessa here?"

Tammy sounded put out as she answered, "Are you serious, dude? Come on. She's a busy person."

I sat there, unsure if I should go out there to see who was asking for me. I didn't want to step foot out there if some weirdo wanted to see me.

"Can you just tell me if she's here or not?" he asked, sounding a little aggravated. "What are you, the Hamburger Hut police?" He sounded attractive, with a deep voice and a Texan accent. His voice sounded sort of familiar too.

"No, I'm just a potato sack-wearing girl with nothing better to do, you jerk."

*Potato sack?*

I jumped up as I suddenly realized who she was talking to. Pushing the swinging door open, I walked out behind the counter. "Tammy, please try to talk in a more respectful manner." I did not know why she had to be rude to the man — we were already on thin ice with him after the cockroach incident.

"Mr. Nash, it's a pleasure to see you again." I hoped it was going to be a pleasure and that he wasn't there to let me know he would be suing us.

"What's this mister crap?" His blue eyes twinkled as he smiled at me. "Jessa, can you take a break?"

I could do anything if it meant he wouldn't be stirring up trouble for me at my job. "Sure, Stone." I was starving anyway. "Tammy, tell Bob to make me the usual." I looked at Stone. "It's on the house if you care for anything. Anything at all."

He held up a bottle of water he'd brought in with him. "I'm good."

Walking out from behind the counter, I set my eyes on a table in the far corner. "You don't even trust our bottled water, huh?"

"Not even a little." He walked next to me, so close that our arms grazed.

A spark shot through me — I assumed it was a result of static electricity. "Oh! You shocked me."

"Did I?" He hadn't seemed to have noticed the little shock that had passed between us.

"Static electricity." I took a seat while he took the one across from me. I wore my ugly uniform, and he was dressed in a pale blue pullover and some jeans that fit him oh-so-right. "You look a lot better than you did last night."

"About last night. I'd like to apologize for anything I may have said. To be honest, I don't recall everything we talked about. So, if we could strike that night from our record, I'd be extremely thankful."

"You didn't say anything too bad."

Tammy dropped the tray of food in front of me. "I'd love an apology." She eyed Stone as she ran her hands over her uniform. "You said our uniforms look like potato sacks."

"Oh." His lips formed one thin line as he wore a sheepish expression. "So that's what you were talking about. Sorry about that. I, well, I don't believe they do." He looked at the uniform then shook his head. "Well, I shouldn't have said

23

anything about what I was thinking. That's what should've happened. Sorry. Really, I am. The booze got to me last night."

"Bet that happens a lot," Tammy said as she turned and left us.

I wished my flushed face would cool off so he wouldn't notice my complete embarrassment. "Kids, huh? So quick to speak their minds."

"Drunk guys seem pretty quick to speak their minds too." He reached over, touching the back of my hand as I reached for my burger. "If I said anything that put you off, please forget about it and know that I'm not that guy."

"Done." His hand on mine made my stomach tense and my toes curl inside my non-slip work shoes.

Removing his hand, he smiled, happy with my answer. "I told you that I'd be back every night until you agree to go out with me. I do remember that."

"And here you are. Even though I told you that I have no time to go out with anyone. Do you remember that?" I took a bite of the burger and saw his eyes widen.

"You didn't even check what's inside that first. You really should, you know that, right?"

"I'm really sorry about what happened to your burger, Stone. But I think that was a fluke or something. That's never happened before in all my time working here." I took another bite to prove that I wasn't afraid of our food.

Looking at my tray, he pointed out, "There isn't one healthy thing here, Jessa. What kind of doctor are you going to be if you eat crap like this?"

"As of right now, I'm still unsure. Besides, right now, I only have time to eat crap. When I'm home, I do eat pretty well. You know, sandwiches and such."

"Sandwiches aren't good for you," he said with a laugh. I loved the way his chest moved with the sound.

"I eat once a day in the cafeteria at the hospital. It's in a hospital, so it must be food that's good for you, right?" With the schedule that I kept, I didn't really have the kind of time required to worry about nutrition. "I'm lucky to get a few bites of food into my system as it is. So, I don't worry about what kind it is. Fuel is fuel."

"I'm a chef," he stated. Then he crossed his arms over his chest, looking at me as if what he said should mean something to me.

Which it didn't. "You cook anywhere I should know of?"

The way he dropped his arms and his face fell told me he didn't have a good answer for that. "No. I'm not currently cooking anywhere."

"So, no job then. Want to cook here?" I grinned to make sure that he knew that I was only joking. A chef would never cook in a dive like this.

"No thanks. And I do make money. I just don't do it with my cooking skills."

"Yeah, you look like a man who haa a job. A good-paying job at that." I picked up a fry and dipped it in ketchup before tossing it into my mouth.

Leaning forward on his elbows, he closed some distance between us. "Let's get to why I'm really here, Jessa. The date. When can you find time to go out with me?"

"There is no time for that. I'm not lying to you. I'm not trying to put you off either. I really wish there was time for something like that. But there just isn't."

"Tell me what your average day looks like, and I'll see if I can carve some time out of it." He was so set on taking me out.

My mind was boggled by the man. He seemed to have it all in spades. The great looks. The great body. He looked like he had some pretty good money too. His personality wasn't half bad either. Why he was willing to sit in this greasy spoon just to get me to go out with him genuinely perplexed me.

Eating my fries, I thought about my schedule and if I should speak with him about it. I didn't owe the man a thing. I didn't owe him any explanation as to why I couldn't go out with him.

But then, I suddenly heard myself rambling on before I'd even decided whether I should answer. "I wake up at five, take a five-minute shower just to wake myself up. Then I drive to the hospital and make rounds with whatever physician I can catch up with. Around ten, the rounds are usually done, and I take a thirty-minute break. I eat something in the cafeteria, sometimes resting my head on the table for a brief nap before going to the pediatric ward to help with the newborns. Once a doctor comes to make the rounds and check on the patients, I go with him or her and see how that all works. I do this so I can decide what type of doctor I'd like to be."

"I think you'd make a great pediatrician." He sighed as he looked at me like I was some kind of an angel. "I bet the babies love you."

"Nope. They don't care for me much at all. I've tried holding them, rocking them, even feeding them. They just don't seem to care for me. So, when I'm there, I do the other things in that department. I stock up the formula and diapers. I read patient files. I grab things for the nurses who tend to the babies. I do everything but actually tend to the babies in there."

Shaking his head, he said, "I can't see that."

"I'm not lying to you, Stone. I guess I give off a bad vibe." I didn't know what else it could be. "It's not like I don't care for babies. They just don't care for me."

"You know what I bet the problem is?" he asked, nodding as if he were all-knowing. "I bet you have this vibe of being so busy that you don't even feel like you have the time it takes to sit down and really give a baby a good rocking. No time for cooing at them while feeding them their bottle."

"How do you know so much about babies?" My guess was that he had a few of his own — by a few different baby-mommas, too.

"I've got lots of nieces and nephews. They all love me." Polishing his fingernails on his shirt, he grinned. "I guess I've got a lovable vibe that says I make time for people."

"I'm sure *you* can make time for people. *I* can't. *I've* got a degree to obtain. And you haven't let me finish telling you about my daily schedule, because it doesn't stop there. I work from six a.m. until six p.m., five days a week. When I get off at six, I go straight home and change into this lovely uniform. I have to be here at seven p.m. where I stay until three in the morning. I live five minutes from here, so I go straight home, take a shower — this time I wash my hair and body — before I fall into bed at about three-thirty. I sleep like a dead person for an entire two and a half hours before it's time to get back up again."

"You said that you work five days a week. So that means you have two whole days off, Jessa. You could go out with me then." He looked like a man who'd just found a diamond in a pile of coal.

"You would think so, right?" But he wasn't right at all. "On my days off, I have to catch up on my classes. Not only do I have the intern work that I must do to graduate, but I also have actual classes. I do try to catch up on my sleep as well. On my off days, I allow myself to sleep in until eight in the morning. But from eight until midnight, I'm on the computer, doing my class assignments. So, yeah, I go to sleep a little bit earlier on my days off and sleep in a little bit later. Would you have me give up sleep for this date?"

"Damn." My schedule finally seemed daunting to him. I could tell that by his expression. "I don't suppose it would be called a date if we just cuddled and slept together on your nights off, huh?"

*That actually doesn't sound half bad.*

"While that sounds sort of wonderful, what if sleeping — you know, the actual sleeping — wouldn't be enough for either of us?"

27

The next day, I found myself sitting with my brother Patton at an Asian Fusion restaurant, my mind wandering back to the previous night and Jessa. "So, she's like full of what-ifs. You know what I'm talking about?"

"Who is?" He tapped his finger on the shiny menu in front of him. "And you're supposed to be checking out the food, Stone, not thinking about some girl."

Waving the menu in one hand, I felt slightly offended that he thought I couldn't do more than one thing at a time. "For your information, I've already decided to start off with the pineapple chipotle chili. And the girl's name is Jessa. I told you how I went to see her last night. Can't you remember that?"

He raised one dark brow as if he was a little confused. "You're talking about the night manager of that fast food place?" He shook his head as he looked down at the menu. "And why the chili? I mean, this is Texas, and Texans are pretty devoted to the normal chili style. Putting pineapple into something that sacred just isn't a good idea. This outing is about introducing you to foods you might want to put on the menu of your own restaurant — a restaurant that we all are hoping you'll be opening in the near future, Stone."

"I know you're trying to help, but I'm not about to steal any recipes from somewhere else, bro." Sometimes, I felt as if my brothers didn't know me at all. "I'd like to see how it tastes. I might not go with chili. I might pair the flavors in other ways. You have to think outside the box. Anyway, Jessa's always wondering about what if this happens or what if that happens. I just wish she would stop thinking that way and put her mind to something more important. Like when she can fit me into her insanely hectic schedule."

"How hectic can the schedule of a night manager of a fast food dive be?" He held up one finger to signal to the waiter that we were ready to order.

In no time at all, the waiter was standing at the side of our table, hands clasped behind his back. "What may I get you, gentlemen?"

Patton led. "I'll have the shrimp fajita stir fry, and he'll have the chili."

"They will be right out." With a slight bow, the waiter then turned and left us.

I hadn't realized that in the short amount of time I'd been talking to my brother about Jessa, I'd left out some pretty important facts about her. "She's an intern at some hospital. She's going to be a doctor."

"Sounds pretty respectable. Can't see why you're hot for her, though. That's not usually your type. From what I've seen, you like loose, brainless, and perpetually horny."

He wasn't wrong, so getting offended would've done me no good at all. "And available. But she's none of those things. And yet, I still can't stop thinking about her."

"How'd you meet her?" He looked at the menu. "We should order some more things, Stone. I want you to really immerse yourself in each cuisine. You know, take it all in."

Looking at my menu, I'd been eyeing this one item. "I think I'll order this avocado salsa egg roll. It should go with the chili anyway." I caught our waiter's eyes. "We've found more things we'd like."

Coming right over, he was quick to ask, "What more can I get you?"

"I'd like an avocado salsa egg roll."

"I'd like to try this crab Rangoon southwest wrap. Is that like a flour tortilla?" Patton looked at the waiter.

"It is a flour tortilla."

"Yeah, I want that."

Spinning on his heels, the waiter left us again.

"Feeling rather daring, I must say." It was nice that Patton was taking such an interest in helping me find my footing as a chef.

"I am feeling that way, brother."

"So, do you think I've got a shot in hell with her?" I just couldn't stop thinking about Jessa. "She's got this southern accent, not like ours. It's so different. Sort of a mix between regal and charming. Her voice is soft most times, but it can get stern. I guess that's from the doctor training. I would guess a doctor would need to know how to be stern with their more stubborn patients."

"How much time have you spent with her?" He looked down at the menu again.

"No more food, Patton. What we have coming so far is more than enough." I wasn't about to let him make me fat while on this hunt for the perfect menu items for me. "And just two nights. The first one doesn't even count cause I was drunk. But last night counted."

"Where's she from?" He put the menu down and picked up his glass of iced tea.

"Don't know." I'd had plenty that I'd wanted to ask her, but she'd gotten too busy to talk. "Who would know that there was so much work to be done at a fast food joint in the middle of the night?"

Cocking his head to one side, Patton wore a skeptical grin.

"Maybe she wasn't that busy. Maybe she just didn't want to hang out with you. No offense, but I can't see a woman with those goals looking twice at a guy like you. You're like heartbreak in cowboy boots. You do realize that about yourself, right?"

His words hurt; I couldn't lie to myself. But somehow, Jessa was different. "Patton, I could see myself spending lots of time with this one. There's something so alluring about her. And that's saying a hell of a lot because, so far, I've only seen her wearing that boring old uniform that no one really looks good in. But she does. I know she'd look amazing in anything if she can pull off that outfit."

Steam rolled off the bowls of food that were placed in front of us. "Enjoy." And then the waiter was gone again.

"It looks good." I inhaled the aromas that wafted from the bowl. "The pineapple is there, but just barely. There's a beefy scent, and then the chipotle pepper too. I bet this is gonna be delicious."

Patton spared no time digging into his shrimp stir fry. "Yum! Who would think of adding spicy fajita-style shrimp to Chinese noodles? But what a combination."

I took a bite of the egg roll and nearly lost my mind. "Oh, yeah! Bro, you've gotta taste this. It's a winner for sure." As we shared our food, I began to wonder if I'd stumbled upon something. "I wonder what the carb count of an egg roll wrapper is."

"I bet you can look that up on your cell." Patton took a bite of the egg roll. His eyes closed, and he moaned softly. "You're so right about this."

Looking up the stats on the egg roll wrapper, I was pleasantly surprised. "It says that this one brand of wrappers has twelve carbs, which isn't bad, but it's not awesome either. But they also make egg roll wrappers out of coconut! And that only has six carbs. The sodium in a traditional wrapper is kind of high, at one-twenty. The coconut wins again with ten milligrams of sodium. I bet I could make some really fantastic egg rolls using the coconut version. And they'd be healthier too."

"You would lose the health thing once you fry them," he pointed out. "Going with only healthy foods might not be the best idea."

"But Patton, there are oils that are healthy. Olive oil, coconut oil, and even avocado oil are good oils to fry with. I can do more research to come up with something a health-conscious person can eat." I wanted to stand out in the crowd. "Health has always been important to me."

"I mean, you work out a lot. And you eat right. But I figured you were just doing that to stay sexy for the ladies." He laughed at his little joke.

"Ha, ha." I dipped my spoon into the chili. One taste and I knew right away that I could work with these ingredients in many other ways. "Pineapple and chipotle work well together. I can imagine using this combination on chicken, pork — hell, even fish and shrimp."

"And wrap it all up in an egg roll." Laughing, he thought himself to be quite the comic genius.

"I'm not about to make an egg roll restaurant." I still wasn't sure what I wanted to do, but I had an inkling about the type of food I wanted to serve in any establishment I was opening. "Jessa doesn't eat right. At least not while she's working at the night job."

"So?" He took a bite of the crab Rangoon wrap, nodding away as he chewed it up. "Umm, hmm."

"Another winner, huh?" Low-carb tortillas weren't bad either. Tacos and egg rolls weren't a bad start for a man who'd had no ideas at all. "These things could be made to order. They can be made fast too." My rusty wheels were finally breaking free and beginning to turn.

Patton's eyes lit up. "Hey, like Subway does. You line up the healthy ingredients, and the customer then chooses between a tortilla and an egg roll. And at the end, you roll it all up and fry it for a few minutes. Crispy, hot, and delicious, as well as mostly nutritious. That could work, brother."

"I'd want more than just that." I didn't want to be small time.

"Remember what Tyrell said at the meeting yesterday," Patton reminded me. "Maybe start with just one thing and move on from there. You've got more than *one* thing with this idea. You've got *two* things, and the combinations are nearly endless. Plus, you can set up a shop in the resort in no time at all. Imagine how proud you'll be at next year's meeting."

Opening a real restaurant, even a small one, would mean commitment. I hadn't ever done commitment before. Even the program I'd taken to become a chef hadn't lasted more than eighteen months, but it had still nearly driven me mad.

Slowly, I raised my head, looking my brother straight in the eyes. "What if I don't have it in me to succeed, Patton?"

His smile told me he didn't have the same reservations about me as I did. "Boy, what's your last name?"

"Nash."

"Yeah, Nash. You've got success flowing through your veins. It's just time to let it out, is all. I think it's time to wrap and roll."

I had no idea what he was talking about. "Huh?"

"Wrap and Roll." His head bobbed, as he must've thought that would mean something exciting to me. "The name of your new place. Wrap and Roll. Get it?"

*Hi, I'm the head chef and founder of Wrap and Roll. Oh, hell no!*

## CHAPTER 6
## JESSA

Last night's shift at Hamburger Hut hadn't seemed as brutal as most nights. Maybe it was Stone's brief visit that had made it more than simply bearable. He did have a way of making me smile — that was undeniable.

It would've been nice if we could've talked longer, but I had to plan next week's schedule, and there was the grocery order that I had to get done too. Free time wasn't a thing I had much of. And for the first time since I'd begun this journey of becoming a doctor, I missed having free time — time to do whatever I wanted with whomever I wanted.

Coffee and a chocolate-covered donut helped quiet my rumbling tummy as I sat at a small table in the hospital's cafeteria. With a fifteen-minute break, there wasn't time to eat a whole meal.

"Care if I join you, Miss Moxon?"

Mavis Morgan was in the same classes as I was. "Sure thing, Miss Morgan. Have a seat."

She put down a steaming cup of green tea — I could tell by the scent that wafted my way. She also had an English muffin with nothing spread on top. "That was some scene in emergency this morning, wasn't it?"

"It's not often that you see a man walk into a room with a hatchet buried in his head." I laughed, even though it had been rather gruesome. "And when he said that he'd accidentally done that to himself, I just about fell over from shock."

"I know." A wide smile told me just how insane we all were in the medical community. "Not in my wildest dreams did I ever see a thing like that happening."

"The trouble people can get themselves into never ceases to amaze me." I took a bite of the donut then wiped the chocolate glaze off my lips with a napkin. "I guess some people have too much time on their hands."

"Unlike us." Nodding, as she too knew the hardships of working her way through school, she went on, "I didn't get off work until five this morning. The morning dispatcher at the sheriff's office was dealing with a sick kid. She had to get her daughter over to her mother's house, which put her two hours behind schedule. Today is going to be brutal."

Even with the usual lack of sleep, I just felt better today for some reason. Stone was probably at the heart of it — not that I was about to say a thing about him to anyone. It could never happen anyway, so why talk about it? "I've got the night off tonight, so I can catch up on my sleep a little. Not a lot. Not completely, by any means. But a little. Just enough to keep me going for another few days or so."

"I envy those who don't have to work nights to make ends meet while doing their internship." She sipped her tea. "How wonderful it would be to come from a family who could help to support me right now."

I hadn't told anyone about my family. When asked, I would simply say that I had to do this thing on my own. I never put down my family for that. It was my idea to do things this way, not theirs. "I look at things this way: the hardships only make us stronger in the end."

"That's a nice way of looking at the sleep deprivation and the stress of not knowing if you'll make enough money to cover all the bills and the tuition payments. There aren't many of us who haven't pulled out student loans to get us through this tough time. Besides you and I, I only know of three others who are doing it this way."

"Well, I wasn't willing to throw myself in a hole for hundreds of thousands of dollars, not for anything. If I could find a way to make this work without racking up debt, that's exactly what I was going to do. And working at Hamburger Hut might seem like a waste of my time, but the fact that they pay half my tuition makes it a dream come true for me."

"Exactly." She knew what I was talking about. "If there wasn't the incentive of tuition reimbursement from my job as an emergency dispatcher, I wouldn't stay up nights working there."

"We might have it hard right now, but in a couple of years, we'll be making great money. And while others are going to be broke, paying back all that money they borrowed in student loans, you and I and others like us will be keeping our well-earned money." I just knew my way was the best one for me. "I can see the light at the end of the tunnel, and man, is it bright."

Finishing off her English muffin, she nodded her head in agreement. "Seeing the light at the end of the tunnel is enough for me. So, are you going to go back to North Carolina once you graduate? Or has Texas grown on you?"

Her reminder of where I came from made memories of home flash through my mind. The mansion I'd grown up in popped up first. Then my father, who stood stoically at the foot of the double staircase, filtered into the scene. My sister, a purse draped over one shoulder, ready to go shopping, stood beside our father.

Life back home wasn't what I wanted anymore. My sister and I had never wanted for a single thing. It was as if even dreaming of having something would make it magically appear. And if we actually asked for something, we got one in every color or style imaginable.

Some would think that a wonderful way to live life. But I found it boring. I also found my older sister to be spoiled and bratty. I never wanted to be like her in any way.

I do believe Lily was uppity from birth. She was a demanding child and had grown into an even more demanding adult. If she had to ask anyone for anything more than once, a bitch-fit would soon follow.

Maybe our father indulged us so heavily because of guilt. Not that he had anything to feel guilty over. It wasn't his fault that our mother wasn't in the picture anymore. It was mine — entirely my fault.

I knew better than to do this to myself. I'd seen a therapist for many years to help heal my wounds, to take away my guilt. But all the help in the world wasn't enough to take away the truth. How could it?

Maybe my sister was able to enjoy the benefits of our life because she held no guilt in her heart. But it wasn't just that I couldn't enjoy life the way it was back home, I couldn't stand it.

My father never tried to stop me from leaving home. He never stood in the way of anything I wanted. But I'd seen the sadness on his face when I'd left that day. I could see that he felt he was losing me, almost the same way he'd lost his wife — our mother.

I went back home whenever school was out on holidays. And he'd greet me with open arms, swaying as he whispered in my ear, "So glad you're home, my baby girl."

I knew he didn't mean to make me feel guilty about leaving, but it exploded within me each time I had to leave to come back to Texas, back to school. And all the while, my sister would barely notice whether I was there or not. She was too caught up in her active social life and her favorite hobby, shopping.

Not having a big sister to take the place of an absent

mother was disappointing. Lily might've been the oldest, but she most definitely wasn't the most mature, caring, or nurturing. I took on those roles within our family.

I often wondered how the two of them got on without me. It was me who Lily asked if she wanted someone to tell her whether her outfit looked nice. It was me who told her if the perfume she wore smelled good or bad. It was me who made sure she got to bed when she came in after some socialite party, plastered and barely able to walk.

As for our father, it was me who made sure he took time to eat and rest. He was such a busy man that he often worked right past breakfast, lunch, and dinner. I'd noticed that he'd gained weight, though. I'd noticed that his dark hair had turned grey in what seemed like overnight. And I'd noticed that he was tired, more so than he'd ever been before.

Part of me knew I should've been home more. They needed me. But the biggest part of me knew that I had to make something of myself, or else I could never truly be what anyone needed. And my passion could not be ignored. I'd wanted to be a doctor since I was old enough to know what one was.

Our pediatrician was a saintly woman. Caring, sweet, and so gentle; she'd been the one to spark my dream. I wanted to be just like her. I wanted to take care of people.

"North Carolina is my home. It's my duty to go back. But I don't think I'll stay in the same house I grew up in. I think I'll get my own place. Since being out on my own — even though it's tough — I've grown to love it. My tiny efficient apartment feels more like home than our place ever did."

"You should get your own place for sure," she agreed. "Moving back in with the parents would be a terrible idea."

Smiling, I nodded as I finished my donut then gulped down the remaining coffee. I'd never said enough about my family for anyone to know that it was just the three of us; Lily, Dad, and me. I hadn't told a soul about what I came from. For all they knew, I came from squalor. But the truth was just the opposite.

Back home, I had a bank account that anyone would've been delighted to have. Not me, though. I hadn't worked for a single dime of that money. I wasn't going to spend it the way my sister spent hers. I knew that someday, I would know what to do with all that wealth. Someday, the reason why I was given all that money and what I was supposed to do with it to make the world a better place would become clear. It just hadn't come to me yet.

"Code blue, code blue in ICU," came over the speaker system.

"Break's over." We both got up, dropped our trash in the bin, then hauled our ass to the elevator to get up to the ICU.

"Is it weird that I pray the whole time someone's in code blue?" she asked me.

"I think it would be weird if you didn't." I was a firm believer in prayer — even if I did forget to pray most of the time. "God help whoever is fighting for their life right now."

"God be with them," she added.

# CHAPTER 7
## STONE

Wiggling her finger at me, come hither style, Jessa wore a sexy smile on her plump lips. "Wanna see the stockroom, Stone?"

Her white button-down shirt was untucked from the waist of her khaki slacks, and the top buttons were undone, revealing creamy hills of succulent flesh. I wasted no time getting out of that booth and hurrying to her. "Can't wait to see that stockroom, baby."

Giggling, she took my hand, leading me back into the bowels of Hamburger Hut. "Anything else you can't wait to see, lover-boy?"

"You — naked." Pulling her back to me, I pressed her body between mine and the wall, undoing the rest of the buttons on her shirt. Her breasts heaved up and down as she took rapid breaths of excitement. The lace of her bra felt soft under my fingertips as I moved them slowly.

"We have to get to the back where I can lock the door." Her golden eyes sparkled with fire. "We need privacy." Her hand moved to unbutton my jeans. "We need each other."

Letting her go just long enough that she could take me back to this room where we could get to know each other much better, I inhaled her sweet scent. "You know, for a girl who works in a hamburger joint, you smell remarkably good."

"Thanks." Opening the door to the stockroom, she pulled me inside, and I kicked the door closed. Making sure to lock it, she leaned back on it, her eyes raking over my body. "Strip."

"Bossy." I pulled the t-shirt over my head. "I like that in a woman." I had a bossy side too. "I took my shirt off. Now you take yours off."

Shaking her head, she stepped forward. "You do it."

It was already unbuttoned, so I pushed it off her shoulders, revealing more creamy flesh. "Want me to get that pesky bra off for you, sweetie?"

"Please." Her lips pressed against the side of my neck as she leaned towards me so I could reach around her, unhooking the bra with expertise.

Pushing the straps down her arms, I rid her of it, feeling her big breasts smash against my bare chest. My mouth watered with the desire to taste her. I kissed my way down her neck as I went down to my knees in front of her, taking her tits into my hands. I gazed at the hard nipples before taking one into my mouth.

Her hands moved through my hair as she moaned softly, "Yes, Stone. I need you."

With my free hand, I undid her pants and let them fall to the floor. She stepped out of her non-slip shoes as I pushed her panties down to join her pants in the puddle of clothing at her feet. Moving up her body, I lifted her, and she wrapped her legs around my waist.

I wasted no time ditching my jeans before I sat her on a nearby table. Her arms wrapped around my neck, her hot breath moved over mine, and then our lips met. Fireworks exploded inside my entire body as our kiss grew deep, satisfying, curing all that had ever ailed me. "Your kiss is magic, baby."

"Well, I am going to be a doctor soon." She grinned before kissing me again.

Her hands moved along my back in soft caresses, leaving me breathless. Every way she touched me felt more than amazing. Trails of fire were left in every path she traced with her fingers on my bare flesh. "If I don't get inside of you soon, I think I might burst."

"What are you waiting for?" She scooted her ass to the end of the table. "Take me, Stone. Make me yours."

"Whatever you want, baby, you got it." I pulled her to me, pushing myself inside of her. As we connected, warmth spread through me, and I held my breath, not wanting this feeling to go away, not wanting it to end. "If this could just go on and on, I'd die a happy man."

Soft eyes looked into mine. "Stone, kiss me."

As our mouths touched once more and I made love to her, a fire ripped through me. Our bodies connected so wholly that it defied imagination. We moved like one, somehow knowing exactly the right ways to stroke one another.

It was like we were meant to be together. Like we were born to be with each other and no one else. Like we were soulmates.

My heart pounded in my chest as I felt things I'd never felt before. Things that made me want to fly. Things that made me want to soar high into the sky and never look down or back at what I'd left behind.

Her hair, soft as silk, beckoned me to tangle my hands in it. Her nails raked across my back — I was certain they would leave their marks. She wrenched her mouth away from mine. "Stone, it's about to happen!"

I felt her body clenching all around mine as she gave in to her desire for me. I couldn't help but join her in the climax that had us both making animal noises as our bodies undulated, pulsed. In the end, we were both entirely spent.

A nearby sofa finally came into view, and I carried her to it, lying down with her on top of me, cradling her in my arms. "I'm never going to let you go, Jessa."

Resting her head on my chest, she mumbled, "Don't ever let me go, Stone. Not ever."

I kissed the top of her head before nuzzling it. "Sleep. Rest. I'll be here when you wake up."

Soft snores met my ears, as she'd already fallen into a deep sleep. I smiled as I listened to her. The sounds began to grow louder and deeper. And then, her body began quivering as a loud snorting sound came out of her.

*What the hell?*

I sat up on the couch in my living room. The room was dark. "Shit. I fell asleep."

It had all just been a dream. A wonderful dream, but only a dream.

After lunch with Patton at the Asian Fusion place, I'd gone to a French restaurant for dinner with my brother Cohen. I'd never eaten so much food in my life. And the effects of all that food had me falling into a deep sleep with an amazing dream.

I got up, stretching my body that still felt some residual heat from the tantalizing dream. Going to my bedroom, I went straight for the shower, cleaning myself up so that I could pay another night visit to my sweet dream lady.

The smile wouldn't come off my face as I showered, remembering the things we'd done in my mind. It made me wonder if Jessa might really ask me to go to the stockroom with her that night. I would gladly agree if she did.

By the time I got out of the shower and dressed, it was half-past ten. I figured Jessa wouldn't be that busy at that time of night. So, I headed her way, whistling along with the radio as I drove over to Hamburger Hut.

The parking lot had seven cars in it. I made a note to ask her which one was hers. That way, I would know if she was there. I saw no reason to go inside if she wasn't. And then, I made another mental note to give her my cell number and get hers. That made sense to me. Surely, she could find time to talk to me over the phone now and then.

Walking into the restaurant, I smelled burning grease, but no one was behind the counter. Some yelling was going on in the kitchen area, "Are you stupid or something?" some man asked. "What made you think that you could pour the grease for the fryers onto the hot griddle?"

"I saw Don do it the other day," another guy replied.

"He didn't use this kind. You gotta turn this grill off, then let it cool down before you clean this shit up. Damn, you've got this entire place stinking to high heaven. What if Mr. Samuels comes in? Then what? It won't be me that he fires. It will be you, Tony."

"Okay, okay. I'll clean it up. I'm sorry. I didn't know."

I had no idea where Jessa was, since she normally would've been the one dealing with this. "Um, hello," I called out.

A short, chunky man came out from around the corner and stepped up behind the counter. "Oh, hello. Sorry about the wait, sir. What can I get you?"

"I'm here to see Jessa."

For a moment, he just looked at me as if he was trying to figure out who I was asking for. "What?"

"Jessa. I'm looking for the night manager. Is she here?"

"Well, we're not supposed to tell anyone about the employees. Now, can I get you something to eat or drink?"

"No." I didn't know how to make myself clear with this guy. "And who are you?"

"I'm the night manager, Bill."

"Okay. So, she's not working then. She's got the night off." I was more than a little disappointed.

"I'm not able to tell you that, sir."

I hated this little guy already. "Yeah, I don't need you to tell me that. If she were here, she'd be out here already." I wondered about the surly girl who'd been working the last couple of nights. Maybe she'd see fit to give me Jessa's phone number.

"Where's… um," I'd forgotten the girl's name. "You know, the surly girl who works here? She worked last night. Taylor or Tara or something like that."

"I don't know who you're talking about, and even if I did, I couldn't tell you. No females are working this shift," he let me know.

"Tammy!" I finally remembered. "That's her name. You know Tammy. She's a real bundle of joy, that one."

"Sir, if you're not here to eat, then I don't think I can help you. And I've got work to get to. So, goodnight." He walked away, leaving me standing there.

Chewing on my lower lip, I turned and headed to the door. I didn't like the disappointment I felt. I hated that I hadn't gotten Jessa's number the night before.

We'd been having a pretty good conversation when she suddenly looked at the time and said she had to get some things done. She said she was sorry but had to return to work. And then she was gone.

I didn't like the way things were going. I didn't like the total lack of control I had over this situation. I liked the girl. She liked me. Or so I thought. She definitely smiled at me like she did.

I knew she had little time for me. But I'd take whatever I could get. I'd never felt so desperate for anyone's attention.

Climbing back into my truck, I wondered how I'd gotten this way in such a short time. Whatever I'd become, one thing was for sure — this new guy had some determination.

I drove to the drive-thru, taking the last chance of getting some information on her. Some guy spoke over the grainy speaker, "Welcome to Hamburger Hut, where the customer is number one and so are the burgers. What can I get you?"

I crossed my fingers that I would get an answer as I asked, "Is Jessa going to be working tomorrow night?"

"Yeah," he said without any hesitation.

"Thanks." That was all I needed. I drove away, whistling along with the radio again, feeling happy that I at least knew when I would be able to see the girl of my dreams again.

# CHAPTER 8
## JESSA

The candlelight flickered in the darkness as I settled into my bed after a long session of classwork. The day had been productive, and I couldn't have been happier about all the progress I'd made. Somehow, I'd managed to finish a whole hour ahead of my usual schedule, so one more hour of sleep was in store for me.

I'd lit a lavender-scented candle to help me drift off to dreamland quickly, hoping for some deep sleep to help me start the next day fresh. A slight smile held my lips as I thought about the way I'd been feeling — happy.

It had been such a long time since I'd just felt happy. I'd felt tired. I'd felt stressed out. I'd even felt anxious. But happy hadn't been in the cards for me in years. And the only thing that had changed in my life was the late-night visits from Stone.

I'd only talked to the guy two times, and here I was, smiling away, feeling happy and actually getting a little ahead with my classwork. It was like he was some sort of time-wizard or something. Or maybe it was just that I had this relaxed feeling and could concentrate harder, which had me finishing my schoolwork faster. Whatever it was, I liked it. A lot.

My eyes felt heavy. My breathing slowed. I fell into the abyss of sleep in no time at all.

A warm breeze moved over my body, and I opened my eyes to find Stone standing by the bed. "I hope you don't mind me stopping by unannounced."

"Not at all." I pulled the blanket up. "Care to cuddle?"

Slowly, he pulled his t-shirt off and then dropped his pants, revealing one hefty male member. Climbing into bed with me, he moved one hand along my side, leaving goosebumps on my skin. "I'd like to do more than just cuddle if you don't mind."

"Not at all." My arms closed around his neck, and my lips traced his neckline. "Just promise to be gentle with me. It's been a very long time since I've done anything like this."

"I can be gentle, baby." His warm lips brushed against my collarbone, igniting a sparking sensation in my nether region.

As he kissed his way to my lips, I began to tremble, not from fear but from excitement. I wanted to feel his lips on mine. I wanted to taste him as our tongues danced together. And I wanted him inside of me in a way I'd never wanted anything in my life.

Our bare skin glided together as our bodies moved to get closer and closer until nothing separated us. His erection pulsed at my apex, beckoning me to open and allow him in.

Slipping one foot along the back of his leg, I moaned as our tongues played together and he gently forced his way inside my trembling canal. "Don't be afraid. I won't hurt you."

"I believe you." Gazing into his deep blue eyes, I had no doubt that this man would never hurt me. Not in any way. I could sense his feelings for me were genuine. "I'll try not to hurt you either."

Moving with a slow and steady rhythm, he leaned in to glide his lips along my neck, nuzzling my skin as he whispered in a husky voice, "Try very hard not to hurt me, please. You're the only woman who's ever had this power over me. I need to trust you not to do that."

Our bodies moved in waves like a gentle sea. Moving my hands along his back, I took in each and every tight muscle. It was as if some Greek god had come into my bed, not a mere mortal man.

"You make me feel better than I knew I could feel." My nails bit into his biceps as I arched up to meet his slow thrusts. "You can move faster if you want."

"Why rush this?" His fingers brushed over my waist as he moved his hand down along the side of my leg, then pulled it up a bit, making him go deeper inside of me. "Let's just take this nice and slow, baby. Just the way we're going to take our lives together. Nice and slow. No rushing at all."

"Our lives together?" The idea sounded good to me. "Do you think you can live with a woman who's so busy?"

"Make a few minutes for me on most nights, and I think I can handle it."

"You could move in with me."

"Or you could move in with me." He grinned as he pulled my other leg up, too, moving deeper inside of me.

"I thought we weren't going to rush things." I moaned as he made things inside of me heat up to a boiling point. "Oh, how are you doing that?"

"Magic." He moved a little faster. "You can have your own room at my place if you want to. That way, you won't have to pay rent. You can quit your job too. I want to take care of you. I want you to know that you can depend on me."

All of a sudden, my body tensed. "I don't want to depend on anyone."

Pulling his head back, he looked at me with wide eyes. "I didn't mean that in a bad way, Jessa. I just want to be here for you in all ways."

"I don't want that." My heart began to race. "I want to do this on my own. I don't want any help. Can't you understand that?"

"Not really." He moved in, trying to take my lips. "Just kiss me, and let's not talk."

As soon as his mouth took mine, I could think of nothing else. He made me feel alive. He made me feel special. He made me feel like I could trust him.

Letting everything go but how he was making love to me, I fell into a sexual trance. Nothing mattered but the way our bodies moved together. The sounds of our heavy breathing filled my ears.

Soft groans, moans made by both of us, turned into harsh grunts and slaps as our bodies pounded each others. "I'm going to explode."

"Do it," he said. "Explode on me, baby."

The climax took me by surprise as my body arched and sounds that had never emerged before escaped my lips. "Oh, God!" I couldn't breathe. "Yes!"

*Beep. Beep. Beep.*

I opened my eyes. My cell phone, lying on the nightstand, lit up as the alarm clock went off. "Shit."

My body was hot and shaking from the intensity of the dream. The room leaned as I sat up — dizziness had the room spinning. I held my head in my hands as I took in slow, deep breaths to calm myself down.

It had all felt so real. But as I sat there, trying to bring myself back to reality, it struck me that my subconscious was already at work. I wanted Stone Nash, and I wanted him badly.

Going to shower, I had to make sure my brain, heart, and soul knew that I could not be in a relationship with anyone at this point in my life. I had too much going on to even try to have something with that man.

Most nights, I didn't have any time for anything but grabbing a few hours of sleep. I couldn't be what any man would need me to be right now. It wouldn't be fair for someone to have to deal with my crazy schedule.

I wasn't selfish. I wasn't some dimwit who thought I could make something work for me and Stone. Nothing would work for us. Not yet anyway.

Dreams like this would wreck my days, I knew that for sure. I couldn't be daydreaming about him or anyone. I had to focus, and I couldn't do that if my subconscious was busy falling in love with Stone Nash.

No one had come into my life in the last six years, so why it had to happen now was a mystery to me. All of a sudden, the light at the end of a long tunnel that I'd finally seen seemed to be growing further and further away.

Once I graduated from medical school, I still had to get through three to seven years of residency. Sure, I wouldn't have to take a second job since I would get paid, but I wouldn't get paid that much either. And the hours I would have to put in would be the same as I was putting in now.

I couldn't ask anyone to understand why I'd brought this onto myself. I couldn't ask anyone to love me. Not now. Not even five years from now. Stone was a pipedream.

Even though it wasn't a thing I wanted right now, I knew the right thing to do would be to not talk to Stone when he came to see me at work. If I made it seem like I was too busy to talk, eventually, he'd just stop coming by.

Leaning my back against the cold tiled shower wall, I couldn't believe how my heart ached with the thought. Stone and I had spent a total of a couple of hours together, and there I was, heartsick with the thought of blowing him off.

My subconscious was a real problem. But I would work hard to get control of it. I had to. There was no other choice. Stone wasn't a viable choice for me. Plus, he didn't seem like the kind of man who stuck around long anyway.

*Maybe if I gave him one night, we'd get each other out of our systems and be able to move on.*

I knew that human nature made the unattainable incredibly attractive. But once the unattainable was attained, that attraction grew to be less and less. And eventually, there wasn't enough attraction left to bother with.

There wasn't any time to give to the man. But if I didn't find a way to get him out of my mind, I might end up flunking a class. And I couldn't flunk a class. Or I might end up not doing well with my internship. And I had to do well with that. Then again, I might end up falling asleep at work, and if that happened, they'd fire me for sure. I couldn't lose my job either. It paid for half my school.

I didn't know how to get out of this tight spot. *Give in to my desires, and risk way too much. Not give in to my desires, and still risk too much.*

Nothing made sense. My world seemed topsy turvy. And it was all that handsome Stone Nash's fault. I already rued the day he'd stumbled into Hamburger Hut and stolen my damn heart.

Shaking my head, I had to rid it of that idea. "He hasn't stolen your heart. It's just lust. It's just an attraction. There can't be any real feelings. You don't even know each other enough to figure out if you actually like him. He's nice to look at. He's built like a brick house. And he's charming in his own way. Just calm the hell down."

I wasn't one to talk to myself, so that was out of character for me, and it bothered me a bit. I wasn't the type of person who let others affect me much. I did my own thing. I was my own person. I didn't need anyone. And I sure as hell didn't need this man getting into the deep crevices of my brain, trying to pull me away from my main goal in life — becoming a well-respected doctor.

*I could just give in and get things over with. I'm sure that'll work for us both.*

But what if a few hot times aren't enough for either of us?

## CHAPTER 9
## STONE

I'd never felt so pumped for something as simple as going to talk to a girl since I was a kid in grade school. But just as I pulled into the parking lot, I noticed a big truck coming in behind me. It went around to the back of the place, and I had this sinking feeling that the arrival of that damn truck would keep Jessa busy for quite a while.

Sitting in my truck, I watched and waited for the delivery truck to leave. An hour later, it finally left, and I got out, still unsure if Jessa would be free to talk to me anytime soon.

Tammy stood behind the counter, the lackluster smile plastered on her face faded as I walked inside. "She's busy, Romeo."

"I'll wait." Taking a seat in a booth in the back, I pulled out my cell and looked for a game to play so I could pass the time.

Before the game had even started, I heard a terrible crashing sound coming from the kitchen, followed by a horrible howling noise. Tammy sprinted around the little partition. "What the hell's going on back here? Oh, God! Josie, what did you do?"

More wailing followed, then Josie whimpered, "I burned

the shit out of my hand. I knocked the damn seasoning off the top shelf and onto the hot grill, and when I tried to pick it up, it slipped. Then I tried to grab it with my bare hand, and I ended up planting my hand on the grill instead."

"Are you okay, Josie?" came Jessa's voice. "I heard all kinds of racket out here."

Josie's voice trembled as she said, "I've burned my hand, Jessa. Look."

"Let me get the burn gel," Jessa said. "Tammy, see if you can find a cook to come in tonight. Once I treat her burn, Josie's going home. Josie, come to my office with me so I can take care of you."

"Great, so I have to make calls to the three other cooks at eleven on a Friday night." I watched her as she went to the corner near the drive-thru window and picked up the phone that hung on the wall. Running her finger down a list of what I assumed were employee's phone numbers, she stopped on one then punched the numbers into the old-timey phone. "Ancient piece of shit." Tammy had her usual crankiness going on. "Hey, Troy, can you come work?"

I watched her shoulders slumping and knew Troy wasn't giving her the answer she was looking for. And when she put down the phone without saying another word, I got the impression he'd even hung up on her. The two next calls weren't even answered, and she freaked after the beeping sound of someone at the drive-thru startled her. Her eyes went to the little pile of burgers that lay wrapped in yellow paper under a heat lamp.

I couldn't just sit there and do nothing. I had to at least offer my help. So, I got up, shoved my cell into my back pocket, and walked up to the counter. "I can help out."

She looked at me with skeptical eyes. "Sure you can, lover-boy." She pushed the button on the speaker. "Welcome to Hamburger Hut, where the customer is number one and so are the burgers. What can I get you?"

"I'll have six cheeseburgers, six large fries, and six Mountain Dews," the customer said, then added, "Oh, and six apple pies. And can you make sure they're freshly fried for us?"

I counted four ready burgers in the little pile under the heat lamp. There weren't many fries ready either. The place where I assumed fried apple pies usually waited was empty. Tammy was in a pickle. "Let me help. I can cook. I am a chef, after all."

"I don't see what choice I have. Come on back here. The aprons are over there." She pointed at some grease-spotted black aprons hanging from a nail on the back wall. "I keyed in the order, so you'll see it on the screen that's hanging to one side of the griddle. I need two burgers to add to what I've already got, and while you make them, I'll get to the fries, apple pies, and drinks."

I'd only had one burger from this place. And since there had been the extra critter in it, I hadn't even had a chance to see what was inside. "Do you guys put everything on the burger or what?"

"Meat, cheese, ketchup, and mustard is all they get if they don't specifically ask for veggies." Tammy raced around, getting the fries and pies into fryers before she got started on the drinks.

I had the little burgers ready in a flash, then started bagging up the order. Another beep came from the drive-thru, and at the same time, the door dinged as it opened, and four people walked in. "Crap," Tammy hissed.

"I can take these guys' orders while you take the one at the window. Then I'll go back and start cooking everything up. Don't panic." I'd worked for a short time at a fast food place back home in Houston when I was a teenager. I thought it had to be a lot like riding a bicycle — once you learn how to do it, you never forget. "Hi, welcome to Hamburger Hut, where the customer is number one and so are our burgers. Or something like that. What can I get you?" The computer screen made it so easy that even a monkey could've run it. *I have this in the bag.*

Slurring a little, the first girl in the line said, "Chicken fingers."

I looked at the screen. "Four or six pieces?"

She looked over her shoulder at the other girl. "How many should I get? Do you wanna share?"

"Get six, girl," her friend said. "I'm starving."

She turned to look at me. "Six." Smiling, she seemed to have finally really noticed me. "Hey! You're cute. Like really hot. When did you start working here?"

"I don't work here. I'm just helping out for a bit. Been partying at one of the clubs around here?" I pressed the six-piece chicken fingers button on the screen, and the amount of money it cost popped up.

"Yeah, we were at Spangles and Spurs. It was ragin', man. But," she jerked her thumb at the girl standing behind her, "this one got the munchies. So here we are. I'm gonna want some cheese sticks and onion rings too."

"What sizes?"

"The big size." She hiccupped. "And some coke as well. Large." She pulled a little silver flask out of the pocket of her baggy cargo pants. "We'll be making our own cocktails if you care to join us."

"Not sure that's allowed." I keyed in her order. "Sixteen fifty-five."

"Wow, that's pretty high." She pulled out a credit card from another pocket on her many-pocketed pants. "But okay."

"It's the cheese sticks that cost so much. I guess they think they're the best ever around here." I swiped her card. "Here you go. Your order will be out as soon as I can get it for you."

"See you at our table soon, handsome." She walked away, making sure to shake her bony ass.

"Okay, I need some food, and I need it now," the next girl in line said with such sassiness it nearly made me laugh.

"K. Tell me what you want, and I'll do my best to get it to you fast."

"A burger. And not just one of those plain Jane's you guys make either. I want it all. Grilled onions. Jalapenos. Add some of that special sauce that you put on that specialty burger that came out last Christmas. That shit is the bomb. And run that bitch through the garden too. I want all the veggies. And don't be skimpy with anything. Oh shit!"

She startled me with her sudden cursing. "What?"

"Bacon. Don't forget the bacon, man. And some fries, and the biggest lemon-lime drink you got." She put her credit card on the counter. "Hook me up, player."

"Consider yourself hooked." I keyed in all the things she'd said, then ran her card, feeling like I was kicking ass at this. "Next."

Tammy rushed up behind me. "Get behind that grill and get cooking. I'll take their orders now."

"Cool." I went back to the kitchen, finding so many orders on the screen that I froze for a moment. "No. I can't do all of these."

Tammy must've heard me because she shouted, "Just get to work!"

"Okay, geez." I took one order at a time, making sure to get everything just right. More beeps came, signaling more drive-thru customers. The door dinged more often, informing me that more people were coming inside. And I just kept cooking, cranking out the food as fast as I could — with a little sloppiness, as I had to rush.

"Stone?" I heard a familiar voice.

"Jessa. Yeah, it's me." I glanced at her. "I'm swamped here. Can we talk later?"

"I can see that." She put on an apron. "Tammy should've told me she couldn't get anyone to come in. I'll take over back here on the grill."

"How about you just help me out?" I pointed at the veggies

that were nearly out. "Can you cut up some more of those for me?"

"Yeah, sure." She went to work, smiling away as she did.

I began to smile too since she was around. "This isn't as easy as I remembered from when I was a teenager."

"You worked in fast food?" She poured some more pickles into their place in the condiment line.

"For a year or so. Mackey's, the place was called. We sold all sorts of things, too. It could get crazy. Just like this." I wrapped up a burger then tossed it into a bag. "Order up."

Tammy grabbed the bag then added the other things before giving it to the waiting customer. "Not too shabby, Romeo."

"Thanks."

Time flew by as customers kept coming. And then some guy came in, took an apron off the wall, and said, "I got it, Jessa."

Jessa pulled me back. "The morning shift has arrived. We're free to go, Stone."

Taking off the apron, I put it back from where I'd gotten it. "Man, I was in the zone. I got lost in there, didn't I?"

"You did." She took my hand, pulling me out of the kitchen. "Thanks for the help. I'll be sure to put you into the system so you can get paid."

"Tell you what." I looked at our clasped hands, liking the way hers fit mine so perfectly. "Add my time to yours instead. You can take my pay. I don't really need it."

"I can't do that." She led me out of the door, into the still dark parking lot.

"Well, I can't take the money. Consider it a favor for a friend." We stopped in front of a little blue car, and she opened the door. "So, this is yours?"

"Yeah. I know it's not much. But I did buy it with my own money. It's paid for." She got into the car. "I'm sure that wasn't

58

how you planned to spend your night. Go home and get some sleep. I'm sure you've got things to do today."

"Yeah." I couldn't stop looking at her as I held the door. "You working again tomorrow?"

"You mean tonight — and yes, I am. But you can't come and be our cook every night without being hired first." She laughed. "I've gotta get home and get some sleep before I go to the hospital. Thanks again, Stone."

"You're welcome." I closed the door, watching her as she pulled out of the parking spot.

She'd almost got out of the parking lot when I remembered that I had originally come to get her phone number. Sprinting after her, I finally caught up just as she was about to exit onto the road. Banging on her window, I clearly startled her.

She rolled down her window. "Stone, what in the world?"

"Your phone number. That's why I came here in the first place. Can I have your number?" My heart beat so hard, making me realize that I was very nervous. "Please."

"Stone, what if you call and I'm too busy to answer, and then you get annoyed with me?"

# CHAPTER 10
## JESSA

"Jessa, have you ever noticed how many times you've asked me questions that begin with what if?" Laughing, he shook his head. "What if you *are* too busy to take my call? I'll tell you the answer. I'll understand. And just so you know, I'm never too busy to take a call or a text from you. Just hearing your voice or knowing that you're thinking about me will bring a little ray of sunshine to my days and nights."

"I've thought about you," I didn't know why I said it. I hadn't meant to.

"And I've thought about you. I've thought about you a lot. I know you're busy. I can see that." He leaned on the window, bringing his face close to mine. "You can trust me to respect your time, Jessa."

"It's not you, Stone. It's really not. I genuinely like you. I've explained my time restraints to you. I just don't think you're fully comprehending them. I've got so much on my plate, and it won't be ending anytime soon."

"You should be graduating in a couple of years. Sounds like your time will be freed up after that," he sounded optimistic and remarkably patient. "I can deal with that."

Shaking my head, I had to let him in on how many more

years there would be with me being short on time. "After grad school, there's residency. And that can take anywhere from three to seven years before I become a real doctor. I'll be making money, and I won't have to make any more payments. But the thing is that I'll be working between seventy and eighty hours a week, much like I do now. So, not much will change." I knew that sounded daunting, and I wouldn't have blamed him if he'd just walked away.

"Jessa, let's just exchange numbers and see how that goes for now." He pulled out his cell. "Put your number in here."

I didn't have time to argue, so I put in my number and he took the phone, calling me right away. "I'm right here, silly. Why call?"

"So you can put my name to that number, silly." He laughed. "It's that easy. Now go home and get some sleep."

I added his name to the number, a bit worried about how this would impact my life. I felt like it would make a huge impact, and I wasn't sure I could really deal with that. "You do the same, Stone. Thanks again for all your help."

He took a step back from my car, waving while smiling sexily. "Not a problem at all. Night, girl."

"Night." My heart sort of sputtered in my chest as if it didn't want me to leave. But I had no choice. I had to get home and get some rest.

My head was in a fog, thinking about Stone and how he'd helped me out in a jam. I didn't know many men who would do such a nice thing for someone they barely knew. It seemed that he was somewhat of a miracle man.

Pulling into my parking spot at the apartment complex, I saw the screen on my cell light up. Picking it up, I already knew who would be texting at this early hour in the morning.

**- You're the most beautiful woman in the world, and I feel lucky just knowing you. Have sweet dreams. -**

Holding the phone against my chest, I went inside my little

efficiency apartment like I was walking on a cloud with stars in my eyes and fireflies filling my mind. I couldn't recall a time I'd felt so light, free, and happy.

*One text, and he's made my day already.*

Pulling my clothes off as I walked into the apartment, I thought about what I should text back. Still on the fence about whether I should give in or hide away from the man, I laid on my bed, staring at the ceiling as if waiting for an answer to magically write itself out on it. "Tell me what to do, Mom."

I'd never even heard the sound of my mother's voice, not that I could remember anyway. I was sure that I'd heard it while still in her uterus, but other than that, I knew there had been no other chances for that to have happened.

My sister, Lily, would've told me to stop being so stupid and go for it already. My father would've told me that it was my decision to make, and mine alone. But what my mother would've told me was a mystery that could never be solved.

It began to bother me that I'd made no real friends since coming to Austin. I had the people I took classes with and the ones I interned with. But I wasn't close enough to any of them to ask what I should do about a man who'd stumbled into my life, my head, and even my heart.

Back home, in North Carolina, I'd had friends. But not the kind that I trusted much. The social circles my family was a part of dabbled in rumor spreading, and gossip was the key topic of any conversation. I didn't dare speak my mind in front of any of them. And I certainly didn't think there was even one of them who I could call to ask for advice about Stone.

The very first thing any of them would do would be to Google his name. That was what they did. They had to find out every little deep dark secret they could. And when they were through with search engines, they'd take their search to social media. It was as if they were all a bunch of nosy reporters who worked for some gossip television show.

I was on my own in deciding to try and incorporate this

man into my life or shut him down. And whichever I chose, I would have to make even more decisions about how I would follow through.

There were more than a few ways to get him to stop pursuing me. The obvious one was that I could simply have sex with him, thus ending his campaign to get into my pants. It would most certainly be over if I did that.

But then again, it might not work out that way at all. It might only make him want more and more from me. And I had little to give. We would end splitting up on bad terms, and I'd feel like everything was my fault — because it definitely would be all my fault.

With a huff, I pulled the blanket over me and stared at the phone. I had no idea what to say to him. I had no idea what I should even do about this mutual attraction we shared.

Finally, I texted him back.

**-You flatter me too much. Go to sleep. -**

Placing the phone on the nightstand, I sighed. I sucked at romance. But I supposed that he should know that about me right from the start. I wasn't one to come up with sweet words to say or write to him. I wasn't one to figure out how I could spend time with him. I wasn't a good girlfriend, and I might never be.

If Stone Nash was smart, he'd forget about me. I would only disappoint him over and over again. Just as I was sure I'd disappointed him with my vague reply to the sweet text he'd sent me.

I might've been as smart as a whip where medicine was concerned — something my high grades proved — but I was as dumb as dirt when it came to romance. Maybe that was because I hadn't been raised in a home with a mother and father who loved each other. I had no role models to show me how romantic couples made things work.

Lily had had a few years of observing our parents in a loving relationship, and I assumed that was why she felt confident in the love department. Although she'd never found the one man for her. Instead, she'd found herself many men, never giving any of them the chance to settle her down.

In the few romances I'd had, we always drifted apart, as I had more important things to do than spend time cuddling. There were no arguments at all. We'd just silently let it go and move on.

*Damn, I'm a sad case, aren't I?*

My father loved me. I was sure he did. And my sister loved me too — in her own way. And I loved them. So, love wasn't foreign to me. But somehow, it had never formed between me and any of the men I'd dated.

I didn't like to think myself incapable of anything. And being incapable of loving someone other than family wasn't sitting well with me either. But, once again, I had to remind myself of how little time I had to offer. And how that would end up disappointing Stone, and he'd end up doing what the rest of the men in my life had done. Silently slip away.

*Better not to love at all if it will only end in pain.*

Closing my eyes, I felt the sharp sting of tears forming behind my closed lids. Crying wasn't something I did often, and I'd be damned if I was going to cry over something so fleeting as this thing Stone and I had going on between us.

Sleep was the only thing I needed to be thinking about. I had to calm my mind so I could get some rest before the alarm went off and I lost any chance of getting so much as a wink of sleep.

Grateful that I wasn't a doctor with patients who would depend on my sharp wits and snappy mind yet, I took solace in the fact that I was only an intern and no one expected great things out of me. But I couldn't do this every day. I couldn't have my mind on Stone and still manage to do and learn what I needed to so that I could become a doctor.

One thing the Moxon family never did was let others get in the way of their progress. My father had taught me that. He'd never remarried or even dated after my mother's death. He'd said that there had only been one true love for him, and his heart had gone with her when she left.

Perhaps mine had too. The love a child has for their mother must be the deepest connection a person can have. And since I had no mother to connect with, maybe my heart didn't even know how to love appropriately. And if that was so, then that was just one more reason Stone should forget about me.

My phone buzzed with another text. My eyes sprang open, and I grabbed my phone.

**- Shoot me a text when you know what time you'll be taking a break at the hospital, and I'll come to join you. And make sure you put in which hospital it is. I can't wait to see you, XXOO. -**

*What if Stone's the one man I could fall in love with, and I'm squandering our time by not making up my mind?*

# CHAPTER 11
## STONE

"Yeah, I'll meet you at Zanzibar at around one, Baldwyn. Middle Eastern cuisine sounds good to me. And thanks for helping me out with this — I feel like I'm that much closer to finding my true calling." I pulled into the parking garage at Travis Memorial, where Jessa had finally told me she interned.

"Whatever I can do to help, bro. You know that. I'll meet you there then. So, what're you doing right now?"

"I'm going to hang out with this girl I met a few days ago. Her name's Jessa, and she's a pretty busy young lady, so I have to grab time with her when she's got a few free minutes to spend with me." Parking my truck, I turned off the engine and got out.

"Sounds weird," Baldwyn said. "When someone likes you, they usually *make* time for you."

"It's not like she's got room in her schedule. I get it. I really do. Anyway, I'm gonna get off the phone now. See you later." I ended the call before I had to defend why I was spending my time on a woman who had no real time to give me back.

It wasn't like I could explain it to anyone anyway. There was just something about her that kept pulling me in. Her presence alone did amazing things for me. But no one would truly understand that. My brothers and friends would all just say that I was itching to get into her pants. And I sort of was, but there was more to it than just that.

Not every woman I'd had sex with had given it up so quickly. I'd had to work at it with a few of them. Once I'd gotten what I was after, I'd lost interest pretty quickly. In my defense, not even one of them had what Jessa had.

From the sound of her voice to the sparkle in her eyes, she gave off such a great vibe. She'd make a great doctor; I was sure of that. The fact that she actually cared about people was evident by her demeanor and actions.

Popping into the lobby, I saw a woman standing behind a desk and walked up to her. "Can you point me in the direction of the cafeteria, please?"

"That way," she pointed to the hallway on the right.

"Thanks." I took off in that direction and then continued following the signs from there. As soon as I turned the corner and walked into the room, I saw Jessa sitting at a small table, looking down at her phone. Sneaking up behind her, I ran my arms around her from behind and planted a kiss on her cheek. "Hey, you."

"Stone," she whispered. "What are you doing?"

"Stealing a kiss." I took the seat across from her. "I figure if I'm gonna get any at all, I'll have to steal 'em."

"I'd hate it if rumors about me began spreading around." She looked around and seemed relieved to find that no one was staring at us. "Well, no one's here, so I guess it's okay."

My lips tingled from the brief kiss. "I think it was a little more than just okay. My lips are on fire over here." I winked at her.

A blush covered her cheeks, and she ducked her head shyly. "You are such a flatterer."

"It's not flattery if it's true, honey." I saw a woman coming our way and then place a plate of food covered in cream gravy in front of Jessa.

"Thanks," Jessa said, then quickly began digging in. "I've only got fifteen minutes of my half-hour break to go. So, don't think me rude if I devour this while you talk."

"What is it?" I tried to make out the food under the heavy coating of white crap.

"Chicken fried steak." She took a bite, nodding as she chewed it up then swallowed. "Well, it's most likely soybeans, not real steak. But it'll fill me up, and that's exactly what I'm looking for."

She took another bite, which I noticed was mashed potatoes. "Are those real or fake too?"

"Fake." She pointed her fork at the small bowl with a greasy sheen on top. "Those green beans are real."

"And really covered in grease. Jessa, you can't eat this terribly every day. I'm shocked that you're in such great shape with this diet." I couldn't believe she wasn't as big as a house with all the junk she ate. "It says a lot about your metabolism. But if you keep eating like this, it will catch up to you one day. I'm gonna start bringing you something to eat. Something healthy."

Pausing, she looked at me as her fork hovered over her plate. "Really?"

"Yes." I couldn't pretend not to care about the crap she was putting into her body. "I'll start bringing you something when I come to see you at work too. I can't sit idly by and let you do this to your digestive system. It would be a crime."

"You're serious, aren't you?" She scooped up some shiny green beans.

"Extremely serious." I knew I had to take a look at what the cafeteria was serving. "Do they serve anything nutritious here?"

"There's salad. And they have mixed veggies. I don't like them, though. They're soggy and tasteless."

"I'm sure they've cooked all the nutrients out of them anyway if they're soggy. Vegetables should be crisp, even after

68

they've been cooked. And if you must use oil with them, you should only use an oil that's low in saturated fats, like olive oil. You would think they would know that around a hospital, of all places."

Shrugging, she didn't seem to have ever thought about that. "You sound sort of passionate about this, Stone. You said you're a chef. Why not come up with an idea to end this madness?" She laughed as if it was a joke.

"You're right. I should." I'd had no idea there would be a need for a place that sold healthy food in a hospital. "Are there any other places to eat in here?"

"We have a coffee shop on the third floor. It's sort of like a Starbucks. You know, various coffees and teas and assorted sweets." She took a drink out of a giant mug.

"And what are you drinking?" I hoped it was water to help wash the crap she was eating out of her system.

"Soda." She smiled impishly, knowing that it was far from healthy. "I know that soda's bad for you in many ways. But I need a little pick me up now and then."

"Sugar is the worst thing to use for a pick me up. You know what's good at doing that? Nuts and berries, proteins of most any kind will do that little trick without causing your digestive system any distress in the process." I knew I would have to bring her more than just a meal when working at the hospital. "I'll pack you some snacks too."

"I can't carry around a backpack full of food, Stone." She finished the food left on her plate. "I grab something when I get the chance to. And every time I leave something in the fridge of the break room, someone else snatches it up. There are a bunch of food thieves up here."

"And I know why that is too." Why wouldn't people be trying to get something better than what this place had to offer? My wheels were spinning, but not the way I'd meant them to be. "Let's talk about something else. I didn't come here to trash-talk your cafeteria. So, your accent — it's not from Texas."

"You're right. I'm from North Carolina."

"What city in North Carolina?" I asked, as she'd been too vague for my liking.

"Around Durham." Leaning back in her chair, she took a deep breath, most likely because the food wasn't settling right. "I'm sorry, Stone. It's time for me to get back to work."

I'd taken up too much time going on about the shitty food. "Damn. I've wasted our precious time, haven't I?"

"Not in my opinion." She stood up, taking her plate to the trash. I got up and followed her. "It sounds like you've come up with something you'd like to do about how so many people only have unhealthy choices available when they're working. And having a chef bring me brunch sounds amazing. Your visit went well, that's what I think."

"I think I might be coming up with a great idea. And if you could help me with it, say as a consultant from the medical field, you could quit that night job, and I could pay you for your help. I'd pay you better than they do, I promise." There was more than one reason why it would make me happy to have her working with me instead of at that crappy night job.

"There's a reason why I have that job, and I can't quit it. Otherwise, I'd lose too much. Plus, I can't see how I could help you with much since I'm not fully trained yet. I wouldn't want to give my uneducated opinions on anything. But it's nice of you to offer."

It shouldn't have surprised me that she would turn me down, but it did disappoint me. "Maybe you'll change your mind once I get something going."

"Don't count on it. I've got things set up for myself, and I'm not likely to change a thing." Walking toward the exit, she asked, "So, will you be stopping by Hamburger Hut tonight?"

"I will. And don't eat a damn thing from there. I'm going to bring you something to eat. Maybe you'll fall in love with my

cooking and figure out ways to spend more time together."
Taking her hand, I stopped her, pulling her closer to me. "Do
you have any favorite types of food?"

"Haven't you noticed that I'll eat pretty much anything
that's available to me?" Brushing her hair back off her
shoulder, she looked at me with shining eyes. "This was nice,
Stone. I mean that. And you've given me something to look
forward to. I like spending time with you."

"Me too." It was nice to hear her say that. "I was worried
that I might be bothering you a bit."

"The only thing that bothers me about you is that I can't
seem to fit you into my schedule. But I'm gonna try harder to
see what I can do about that. If you can give me time to figure
that out."

"You've got all the time you need, baby. I ain't goin'
nowhere."

Smiling with only half her lips, she whispered, "I knew I'd
like hearing you call me that. You're something else, Stone
Nash."

"So, you're not into calling me something sweet yet?" I had
to be patient with this one. "That's cool. I'll grow on you.
You'll see. You'll be calling me babe, sweetie, and honey before
you even realize you're doing it."

"Think so?" Smiling slyly, she started heading to the exit
again. "We'll see. I've never been one to talk like that.
Romance hasn't been my strongest suit."

I was glad to hear that, in a way. It meant she'd never been
in love before. And I hadn't either. Not real love. We could be
each other's first and, hopefully, last loves. If everything
worked out.

"Bet I can change that." I would do my damnedest to get
her interested in romance and all that it implied.

*Maybe he could change that.*

He'd stolen a kiss from me, so I thought I'd steal one right back. About to part ways, he let go of my hand, and I reached out, touching his cheek before placing my lips on his other cheek for just a second. The tingling sensation that was left on my lips made me smile. "See you tonight, then."

He couldn't wipe the smile off his face. "Tonight. Don't eat. Don't forget. I'm gonna knock your socks off with what I bring you."

"Can't wait."

"I'm gonna take a look around this place before I take off." He headed in the opposite direction. "My wheels are spinning."

"Good." I turned to find Doctor Weaver looking at Stone as he walked away from me. "Doctor Weaver, what do you have going on right now?"

"I'm about to go scrub up for a tonsillectomy on an eleven-year-old boy. Care to watch, Miss Moxon?" He led the way down the hall.

"I'd love to." I walked alongside him, and a few other interns joined in behind us. "Tonsillectomy," I filled them in.

"Cool," one of them said.

"Miss Moxon, do you mind if I ask you what that gentleman's name is?" the doctor asked me.

"Stone." I wasn't sure why he'd ask about him, but he had eyed Stone a bit. "You know him?"

"Not sure. He does look familiar, though." He led us back to the wing where the operating rooms were located. "I haven't seen him around here before. Do you and he have something going on?"

"I'm not sure yet." I had no idea why he was asking me such personal questions. I didn't much care for it either. "So, we'll go put on surgical gowns and scrub up then meet you inside, Doctor Weaver."

"Yeah, you all go do that."

The other interns were young men, and all of them seemed interested in the questions the doctor had asked me. Toby bumped my shoulder with his as we reached for a gown at the same time. "So, do you have a boyfriend now, Miss Moxon?"

"No." I didn't like this at all. It was exactly what I didn't want to happen. "Can we just stay out of each other's personal lives, please?"

"It's just that it's been years, and we've never seen you with anyone. We were beginning to wonder about you, is all," he clarified.

And I hated that. "Don't wonder about me. There's nothing to wonder about. I'm here to become a doctor. End of story. Nothing to wonder about at all. And if I do have a boyfriend, still nothing to wonder about."

The other intern, Javier, stepped up. "Let's mind our own business, Toby. She's not one to be teased, obviously."

"You're right about that." I put the gown on then went to scrub up.

I detested people talking about anything that concerned my personal life. I wasn't there to be talked about or understood. I was there for one purpose, nothing other than that.

Meeting the doctor just before we went into the operating room, he asked, "Miss Moxon, can you please help me with the mask?" He held his gloved hands up, not wanting to touch anything.

"Of course." I pulled a mask off the shelf.

"That man you were with — you know his last name, don't you?" he asked.

I saw Toby and Javier earwigging on our conversation. "Of course I do."

"It's Nash, isn't it?" the doctor asked with a knowing grin.

"Yes, it is." I had no idea how he knew that.

"Have you been to the resort he and his brothers own yet?"

"The what?" I must have misheard him.

"He and his four brothers own Whispers Resort and Spa near downtown Austin. You knew that, right?"

I did not know that. But the way everyone was now looking at me bothered me immensely. "I know he's a chef. We haven't had time to talk much."

"I bet," Toby snickered. "Doing the horizontal mambo doesn't leave one with much time for conversation."

Snapping my head around, I glared at him. "It's not like that at all. I don't appreciate you saying such a thing."

Doctor Weaver scowled at Toby. "That's not okay."

"I apologize." Toby ducked his head. "Sorry, Jessa."

"Miss Moxon," Doctor Weaver corrected him.

"Sorry, Miss Moxon," Toby said, then went into the operating room, followed by the other interns.

Just before I put on the doctor's mask, he said, "I didn't mean to start up anything. It's just that I was certain that I knew that man from somewhere. The Nash brothers were featured on the cover of Texas Monthly. I think it was in last year's November issue. The men have made billions — they're really starting an empire, it seems. I just wondered if you knew that you were hanging out with a very wealthy man. I meant no disrespect."

My jaw clenched. "I know you didn't." The news he'd given me wasn't good at all.

"You should see if you can find a copy of that magazine. They did a whole spread on all of them. From what I recall, he's the youngest and has a culinary. But he's never opened up a restaurant in the resort. And he's pretty much considered to be a playboy, if you know what I mean. Just be careful. I know you're a very good person, and I'd hate to see you get hurt by anyone."

"Thank you." My face was hot with anger and embarrassment.

The fact that Stone had left out such an important fact about himself bothered me. Granted, we hadn't had much time to get to know much about each other, but I thought he would've said something about being a wealthy man.

As I stood in the operating room, watching the procedure, I couldn't focus. This thing I had with Stone was already interfering with what I was in Texas for. To become a doctor, not some rich man's plaything.

I'd left that world behind me, and I wasn't looking to get back to it in another part of the country. If I didn't know anything, I knew the way the wealthy did things. But the thing about Stone was that he hadn't acted a little bit like any of the wealthy people I'd grown up knowing.

Stone seemed down to earth in many ways. I couldn't even think of one person from back home who would've stepped up to help out at Hamburger Hut the way Stone had.

I had no idea how far he'd go to get into my pants, though. Maybe he was just pretending to be a nice guy who didn't care about keeping up with appearances. Maybe he would do just about anything to get to what he was after.

Trusting him had been a huge mistake. I should've known better. Now the best thing to do would be to completely shut him out. There was no other choice.

The surgery went as expected, and within a half-hour, it

was over. I followed the doctor out, taking his mask off for him. "There you go, Doctor Weaver."

"Thanks." He pulled his gloves off, tossing them into the receptacle. "You should come to my office across the street. I think I've got that magazine over there."

I didn't know if I wanted to read the article. But if I wanted to know the truth about the man, I thought I should read it. "Thanks. I'll come with you when you go."

An hour later, I sat in Doctor Weaver's waiting room with the magazine featuring Stone and his equally handsome brothers on the cover. They all wore black suits, each one of them standing in front of the resort they owned. Smiles on all their faces, they certainly looked happy and proud.

I turned to the page where the article was and began reading.

*Some of Austin's newest sons have brought forth a resort that's caught the attention of people from all around the globe. Baldwyn, Patton, Warner, Cohen, and Stone Nash work closely together to make Whispers Resort and Spa the great success it has become.*

*While the four older brothers run the company, Stone alone has yet to find his place within their sprawling business. As a chef, all thought he would head the first restaurant that opened at the resort. The Micheline star winning restaurant, Essence, has instead been the brainchild of another chef.*

*Many wonder when Stone Nash will find his calling, or if he ever will. Austin's active nightlife seems to be his passion for now. Nearing the end of his twenties, many speculate that Stone's older brothers will soon be forcing his hand. But then again, the billionaire brothers might just allow their equally wealthy youngest brother to just coast through life.*

Closing the magazine, I couldn't read any more of the article that spanned three pages. I'd gotten the gist of it anyway. Stone was a spoiled rich kid, and he would never grow up. He'd have no need to, since his bank account was nice and plump and there was no end in sight as to how much more money would be added to pad his already fat account, I was sure.

He could afford to screw around and not make anything of himself. I knew many who had the same luxury. And I did as well. Only I wanted to make something out of myself. There was no reason to let the rich playboy pull me down with him into the luxurious gutters full of wealthy brats.

That wasn't the way I wanted to live my life. I had left that far behind me, and the last thing I wanted was to find it again out here. Placing the magazine face down on the pile of other magazines on the coffee table in Doctor Weaver's waiting room, I got up and left his office, then walked back across the busy street to the hospital.

I needed to concentrate on what really mattered and stop thinking about that spoiled man. I would put an end to his advances that night. I had no more time to waste on the likes of him.

Heading to the pediatric wing, I hoped to get my mind off him. There was always lots of hard work to do in that area. Going to the nurse's station, I found one of the nurses frowning. "What can I do to help, Shelly?"

"We've got an extremely cranky baby, Miss Moxon. She's got some terrible issues. Her mother used drugs all throughout the pregnancy. The state is taking the baby out of her care. But not until we get her healthy enough to leave us. It's a real shame. She hasn't stopped crying since her birth, which was four hours ago. I know you don't normally get on with the babies, but we need everyone to take a go at this little one."

"I hope I don't make things worse." My mood was as foul as it had ever been. "But I'll try to comfort her."

"Go on back to the last room on the left. We had to put her in a room away from the nursery, as she was upsetting the other babies in there," she explained.

I heard the sad cries before even opening the door. My heart broke for the poor thing. Not only was she suffering from withdrawal from the drugs her mother had pumped into her tiny, developing body, but she was also lost without her mother's presence.

"I'll take her," I told the nurse who rocked and rocked the crying baby.

"Good luck. My heart aches for this poor child." She got up, handed the baby to me, then left, shaking her head sadly.

I didn't sit down. Instead, I took her to the window. The curtains were drawn, but I felt that some sunlight might help her. Pushing one open just a little, a few rays fell across her red face. She was in such a state that her entire body was beet red from all the crying.

"Things aren't as bad as they seem, little one." I swayed back and forth with her cuddled against my chest. "Hush now, don't you cry, momma's gonna sing you a lullaby. Everything's gonna be alright. You'll sleep well in my arms so tight," I sang to her.

Her wailing reduced, and she nuzzled her nose against my chest. I went to get the bottle that sat on the table. As soon as I brought it to her mouth, she took right to it.

I'd done the impossible. I'd calmed her down. Me. The person who couldn't calm any baby down.

*Wow. This is amazing.*

After putting the finishing touches on the stuffed red and yellow bell peppers, I headed to Hamburger Hut to see what Jessa thought of my healthy creation. A mix of Indonesian black rice, farm-raised, antibiotic, and steroid-free chicken thighs, along with chickpeas, turned the pepper's filling into an amazingly delicious and awesomely nutritious meal. Of course, I was biased, since I'd concocted the recipe. I needed Jessa's true opinion before I added it to the menu I'd begun creating.

I still wasn't exactly sure of the size of the restaurant I wanted to open, but I did know one thing — I was going to make healthy foods that tasted great. It was a start, and that was better than no ideas at all.

With the covered tray in hand, I couldn't believe the excitement I felt as I walked into Hamburger Hut. Tammy actually smiled at me as I walked in. "You're back."

"I *am* back." I held up the bag. "I've brought your boss something to eat. Can you tell her that I'm here?"

"We do serve food here, you know."

"This is better, though." I took a seat in a booth in the back, placing the tray on the other side of the table for Jessa.

Tension now crept into my body as I grew a little worried that she might not care for what I'd made.

Tammy came out of the back, shouting across the dining room, "She's working on some reports right now. And she said she's not hungry."

My brows rose as confusion set in. "Not hungry? I told her not to eat anything. How can she not be hungry?"

Tammy came out from behind the counter to take a peek at what I'd made for Jessa. "What is it, anyway?"

"It's stuffed bell peppers. It's a recipe full of superfoods." I'd brought four of the peppers, so I thought I should offer her some since Jessa wasn't hungry. "Bring a plate, and I'll scoop one up for you to try."

Her eyes lit up. "Really?"

"Sure. Jessa probably won't eat them all anyway." I wasn't exactly happy with the way Jessa seemed to be blowing me off. But I'd told her over and over again how patient I would be about her work schedule. I was finding that it was easier said than done.

Racing away, Tammy soon returned with a plastic plate and fork. "Here ya go."

I scooped one of the peppers out of the tray, placed it on her plate, then handed it to her. "Have a seat. I'd like to get your honest opinion on this."

Cutting into it, she inhaled. "It smells delicious."

"Thanks." I waited, watching her without blinking as she took the first bite. I'd made plenty of food for family and friends, but this was different somehow. This might become a part of a menu that I'd serve in a restaurant of my own.

She put the bite into her mouth, chewing slowly. When her eyes closed, I knew she loved it. "Wow." Opening her eyes, she went for another bite. "The way the flavors combine is phenomenal."

I let out the breath I hadn't realized I'd been holding. "It is?" I mean, I knew the taste was great, but she's used the word phenomenal, and that was even better.

Swallowing the next bite, she nodded. "I know I'm only a couple of bites into this, but I like the light feeling it has to it. You know, it's not heavy. But I do feel like it'll fill me up."

"It should. The rice and beans are high in fiber. The fiber is what fills you up. But it breaks down in the best possible way, so you won't feel that uncomfortable full feeling. You know, the way you feel after you eat a hamburger."

"I do know that uncomfortable feeling." She lifted up a forkful of the filling, checking it out. "What's the purple-ish stuff?"

"That's Indonesian black rice. It's sometimes called forbidden rice because of the purple color it turns to when it's cooked. Purple used to be exclusive to royalty, so it was forbidden to normal people and reserved for the Chinese royals." I couldn't believe how excited I was to tell her all about the dish. It felt odd, but in a great way. "Out of all the varieties of rice, that one has the highest antioxidants. I've been reading about a condition in humans called oxidative stress. And that rice helps alleviate it."

"Bet it's expensive," she said with a nod.

"Not too bad. It goes for around seventy-five cents an ounce. To stuff six peppers, I used one ounce of rice. The sixteen-ounce bag cost me a little over ten bucks. I think it's worth the price. Sure, white rice is a little over a dollar or two for sixteen ounces, but it has nothing nutritious about it." Using ingredients with high nutritional value was my main goal.

The door opened with a ding, and Tammy's face fell. "Crap."

"Take it with you," I said as I put the lid back on the tray. "I'm gonna sneak back to give this to Jessa. I can't wait for her to try it."

"If she doesn't love it, then she's nuts." Taking her plate with her, she went to wait on the customer. "Welcome to Hamburger Hut, where the customer is number one and so are the burgers."

I discreetly made my way around the counter, through the kitchen, and into the back hallway. I hadn't been back there, so I felt slightly confused when I found several doors, all of which were closed. "Jessa?"

The sound of chair legs scraping against the floor told me where I could find her, so I went one door down and opened it slowly. "Stone, what are you doing back here?" she snapped at me.

"Coming to give you something that I told you I would." I went inside to find an annoyed expression on her usually smiling face. "What's wrong?" I put the tray on the desk in front of her then removed the lid. "Whatever is wrong, this will fix it."

"You shouldn't be back here. I might get fired for this." She didn't even look at the food I'd placed in front of her.

"I *cooked* here last night. I'm fairly sure if anything could get you fired, that would be it." She was giving off a terrible vibe that I couldn't ignore. "Jessa, what's wrong?"

"Nothing. You should go. I'm too busy to talk to you tonight. I've got loads of work to do." Moving the papers around on the desk, she moved the tray out of the way. "I'm not hungry. You should take that with you. No reason to waste it on me."

There was no denying that her mood was the foulest I'd ever seen. Not that I'd been around long enough to know what sorts of moods she was generally in, but this one took the cake. "I honestly think that you should eat this. You're not yourself right now. I bet it's because you haven't eaten anything. Just try it."

"I said I'm not hungry." Her eyes finally came to mine. "And I'm busy. So just take the food and go."

Generally, if someone was this shitty towards me, I would've left. But something felt off. And I wasn't about to leave without finding out why she was so mean all of a sudden. "Obviously, something happened today after we met for your break that upset you. Tell me about it, and I might be able to help. If it has anything to do with this crappy job, I can fix that. I can hook you up with a job by tomorrow. Even if I couldn't do that, I could just give you whatever money you need until you could get another job."

Slamming down the pen she was holding tightly in one hand, she hissed, "That's the thing with rich guys. They always think they can solve every problem with money."

"Rich guys?" I got the impression that she was upset with me for some reason, but I still could not figure out what it could be. "Jessa, why would you say something like that?"

"I saw the article about you in Texas Monthly. You and your four brothers. You own a resort. You never told me that." Her face turned red with anger as she went on, "The thing with you is that you think you can buy whatever you want, including me. Well, *I* can't be bought."

"I do not…"

She cut me off, "No. *You* just be quiet and listen to what *I* have to say. You only want me because you can't have me. That's all this is, Stone. You're willing to pay me to stop working nights here just so you can have me all to yourself. But I don't want someone to financially support me. I don't want to trade sex for money."

"Jessa, you know it's not like that," I tried to explain.

But she wasn't going to give me any time to explain myself, as she interrupted me again, "It's *exactly* like that. You pay me so I don't have to work this job. And that would free up my nights. You would expect me to spend that free time with you since you would've so generously given me money to pay my bills. Don't act like you would give me money or even a job and not expect me to spend most of my free time with you."

I hadn't even thought about it like that. "Jessa, that's not what I'm doing."

"You are too!" she shouted as she stood up straight, slamming her hands on the desk. "Maybe you don't even know you're doing it because, most of the time, rich people can't see the manipulative things they are doing. I've been honest with you from the beginning, and you haven't been honest with me."

"How's that?" I didn't think I'd been hiding a thing from her.

"You didn't tell me that you own a resort, for one."

"My brothers and I own a resort and spa. There, now I've told you. I wasn't keeping it a secret. We just haven't been able to talk much, with the small amount of time we've spent together." I didn't like being accused of lying or hiding things when I hadn't done that at all.

"The article made you out to be a womanizer. What makes you think that I want to become just another one of Stone Nash's many conquests?" She huffed, pushing her hand through her hair. "And it made you out to be a spoiled brat who's doing nothing at this resort while your brothers do all the real work. Very typical rich guy, if you ask me. And frankly, I'm not interested in being with anyone like that."

*Have I become spoiled?*

Shaking off the thought, I had to defend myself. "I hadn't found my true calling yet. I knew it was something in the world of food, but I didn't know what. Not then. But now — well, now I may have found what excites me about food."

"The bottom line is this," she said as she looked into my eyes with honesty. "You're a crapshoot, a gamble. I could fall for you, and I could have sex with you, but in the end, you would probably get tired of me and my lack of free time. You are who you are — a rich man who hasn't had to work hard at anything or had a problem getting any woman he wanted.

What if I fell in love with you, and then you left me brokenhearted because once you get me, you won't want me anymore?"

# CHAPTER 14

## JESSA

"You know, Jessa, life ain't worth livin' if you refuse to take chances." Stone stared right back into my eyes with defiance. "And you're completely wrong about me. You're making assumptions, none of which are correct."

"I don't think I'm wrong at all." I wasn't going to fall for anything else the man had to say. "Can you honestly tell me that you haven't had the same thoughts as me? What if you fall in love with me, and I don't reciprocate your love?"

Shrugging, he said with stark honesty, "That's a chance I'm willing to take."

"Well, I'm not." I knew the type of man he was, even if he refused to see himself as such. "People who come from money aren't often satisfied with what they possess. They always seem to be looking for what they can get next."

"Let me clarify something for you, Jessa Moxon. I was not born wealthy. As a matter of fact, it's only been a few years since I've had this kind of money. I don't think you can call me a spoiled rich guy, so please, don't do it again."

"You had to come from money for you and your brothers to get into the resort business." I wasn't a fool, and he needed to know that.

"Our cousins inherited money, and they gave us some to start the resort. Now we're all partners in the various businesses we all have. For your information, they didn't grow up with money either. We're all just regular guys who got lucky, that's all." He sat down in the chair on the other side of the desk. "As far as my contributions go, you're right. I haven't done a thing to contribute or boost our company. But I'm on the verge of something. And I brought you something to try. Now, I don't think I want you to try it."

I couldn't let him wear me down. No matter how firmly he believed that being wealthy did not impact one's personality, I knew it to be otherwise. "Look, I just don't want to get hurt. I don't want anyone trying to take what little time I have while not interning or working. Understand it or don't, that's up to you. But I've got to do what's best for me. You should just forget that we ever met."

"Maybe you're right." He looked up at the ceiling as he took a deep breath. Then he looked at me. "The thing is that you've woken something inside of me, and I don't want it to fall back to sleep. I'm different when I'm with you. And just thinking about the little moments we can share has me feeling like I'm floating on the clouds. I don't want that to end."

I had to look away from his blue eyes. Eyes that pulled me in like magnets. Of course, he didn't want the euphoric feeling to end — who would? "It's just the thrill of the chase. Catch me and watch it all fade away."

"Why do you think so little of yourself?" he asked. "And why do you think so little of me? You don't know me well enough to make these kinds of assumptions."

"And you don't know me well enough to know if you're actually attracted to me or merely attracted to something you can't seem to grab hold of."

"You're scared." He nodded as if he knew everything. "I get it. You're afraid of falling for anyone — not just me."

"No, that's not it. And I don't really care to talk about it

87

either. I've got too much on my plate to mess around with anyone right now." He didn't need to know about my mother's passing and how I felt that I was the reason behind it. He didn't need to know that I wasn't even sure if I knew how to love a man the way one's supposed to. But I wasn't about to let him in on the reasons behind that either.

He sat there, staring at the little black tray he'd brought me. "Your shitty eating habits have inspired me. I've changed my mind; you *should* taste what I made you. Tammy had some, and she loved it."

I had no appetite. It wasn't as if it was easy for me to blow him off. I'd been upset with the news of his wealth. Even if he hadn't always had money, he had it now, and I knew he'd already fallen into the same pit that most did.

He didn't know the things I knew about the wealthy and elite members of society. The night we met, he'd come in drunk from a night of partying at a nightclub. My bets were that he'd been all up on various hotties while in the clubs too, spending money like it was as free as air.

"Well, if Tammy loved it, then you have her feedback, don't you? You don't need mine. I'm not in the best mood, as you can see. My feedback might not be accurate. I don't want to spoil this for you. And I can see that I could do that quite easily." He had no idea what it was like to have a passion for something. "When you find your calling, you don't need anyone's opinion. You do it because you not only want to do it, but because you also feel that you must do it."

"I'd like to get back to why you're not in a good mood right now. If it all came from thinking I was some spoiled rich guy, you now know that I'm not. So, your mood should be better now."

It would be impossible to explain why I had such a strong aversion to wealthy men without telling him that I, too, had tons of money. "Yet, it's not. As I have pointed out, there are more things that I'm not comfortable with."

"Yeah, the 'what if I lose interest in you' thing," he said with a grin. "It would be great if you stopped asking yourself and me all these what-if questions. They don't serve any real purpose."

"I think they do serve a purpose," I argued. "I think I'm being realistic."

"Let's see how you handle some what-if questions that I've come up with, shall we?"

Crossing my arms over my chest, I could see that Stone had a tenacious side. "Unlike you, I'd be happy to try to answer any questions you might have."

"Good." He smiled even bigger. "What if our meeting was fate and we're meant to be together?"

I didn't believe in such silly things. "You should know that I think it takes a lot of work to get the things you want. Fate stepping in might seem like a real thing to some, but not to me."

If I believed in these things, then it would mean that all things happened due to fate. If love could occur through fate, then sadness and even death could too. I didn't like to think like that.

"Let me rephrase that question," he said, reaffirming my notion about his stubborn side. "What if, while we're collaborating on my menu project, we fall hopelessly in love and have a happily ever after ending?"

"You should know that I don't believe in happily ever afters. Those are just fictional stories, not real life." I knew about the heartbreak of losing a mother before I even got a chance to know her.

"What if I said that I'd like the chance to make you change your mind?" A low chuckle told me he thought himself clever. "You also didn't respond to part of my question. The one about collaborating with me to come up with a menu. I understand that you think a person doesn't need anyone else to fuel their passion. But you're not being fair about that. Your passion is for medicine. So, what if there were no sick people that you could help, would you still call what you have a passion?"

"There will always be sick people," I countered.

Nodding, he said, "And there will always be hungry people."

Pulling the tray towards me, I removed the lid, since I knew he wasn't about to give up anytime soon. "I had no idea how tenacious you were, Stone."

"There are lots of things that you don't know about me yet. We'll fix that as time goes by. So, what's your first impression of this meal?"

"Honestly, it looks colorful. I know from the nutrition courses I've taken that colorful food means healthy food."

"Ah, so you do know a thing or two about nutrition. You simply don't follow a diet full of nutritious foods." He tapped the desk with his fingers. "Is that because you don't have any available foods that are good for you and taste good while working here or at the hospital?"

"Yep." I pulled a plastic-wrapped fork out of the desk drawer. "I'll give this a taste. From what I see, it looks appetizing. But the real test is the taste. Just because something looks good doesn't mean that it is. From my experience, healthy foods don't have much flavor. Or if they do, it's on the acidic or sulfuric side. I hate broccoli and cauliflower because they taste like sulfur."

"Noted," he said as he sat up, watching me like a hawk. "Be honest with your critique, please."

"Is this supposed to be served at room temperature?" I looked at the microwave on the small table. "Should I zap it first?"

"Don't you dare," he said, shaking his head. "It's good at room temp, I promise."

"Okay then." I went for a bite from the yellow bell pepper

first, making sure to get some of the filling along with it. "Are these chickpeas?"

Eagerness filled his face. "They are."

"Oh." I'd never cared for those. "Okay, well, here it goes." The bell pepper had a slightly sweet taste, the chicken balanced well with the other ingredients, and the texture was good. "A nice crispness to the pepper. I like that. It's not mushy at all. You've used some seasonings that I'm not familiar with. But I like them. And I couldn't make out the chickpeas, so that was good because I don't care for them."

"Would you buy something like this?" he asked with wide eyes as I took another bite.

As I chewed it up, I tried to be honest while remaining objective. I swallowed the bite as I thought about the question. "How much money would something like this cost? Not to make it, but to buy ready from a restaurant."

"The cost of the ingredients was around fifteen dollars. It made six servings. So, it cost me about two dollars and fifty cents for each serving. It took around an hour to make. In most restaurants, it would probably sell anywhere from ten to fifteen dollars, depending on their overhead," he said.

"So, here's the thing. I get a free meal here. At the hospital, I have a budget of ten dollars a day. And that's for snacks and lunch. I couldn't afford this, is what I'm saying. If it was within my budget, I would buy it, though. It's really tasty, and from the ingredients, I can see that it would be a lot easier on my stomach than what I have been eating. And the fact that you can eat it at room temperature and it still tastes good is a winner in my book."

"Thank you," he said, then stood. "I'll leave you to your work then." He turned to leave but then stopped and turned back to face me. "For the record, I've never hung around with any woman long enough to have an argument with her. The fact I wanted to talk things through with you means a lot. Just wanted you to be aware of that. I'm not about to walk away because it gets a little uncomfortable at times. I'll see you tomorrow with something else to eat. Ten-ish again?"

I nodded. He'd kind of blown my mind, and that had left me feeling a little speechless. But then I found my voice. "Just so you know, I haven't had arguments with anyone I've dated. I never cared enough to let them know what I thought about anything they did that bothered me. We would just sort of drift apart. You don't seem to be a drifting-off type of man." A smile pulled my lips up at the corners. "That's kind of cool."

With a wink, he asked, "What if this all works out, and you end up believing in things you never thought you would?"

## CHAPTER 15
## STONE

With one item added to my menu, I felt like I'd finally achieved something. But one item wouldn't be enough. I needed more. So, I made a list of superfoods that packed the nutrients people needed to be healthy.

Nuts and berries, leafy greens and whole grains, cruciferous vegetables and tomatoes, legumes and yogurt, olive oil, and fish; these made up the list of foods said to be super. But these foods alone couldn't make up the dishes I would serve. The food I made had to be as tasty and beautiful as it was healthy.

Going back to the lunch I'd had with Patton, I thought about the egg roll and burrito idea. Those would be foods people could eat on the go, and I could fill them with only the best ingredients. Snack packets filled with nuts, dried berries, dark chocolate chips, and coconut flakes would be an inexpensive pick-me-up.

Ideas started flowing in, and I wrote them all down as I perused the internet for all the information I could get on the foods I would serve. My eyes fell on the clock on my laptop screen, and I realized it was six in the morning.

"Crap, I've gotta come up with something for Jessa and have it there by ten." With only four hours left to come up with an idea, buy the food, then come back and make it, I had to hurry.

Amazingly enough, even though I'd had very little sleep during the night, I was wide awake and raring to go. The usually full parking lot at the grocery store that stayed open all night was almost empty at that early hour. When I went inside and grabbed a cart, I felt like I had the place all to myself.

"Hi," a woman's voice came out of nowhere. "You're up early."

Spinning around, I saw her coming out of a side door near the entrance. "Oh, there you are. Hi. Yeah, I'm beating the crowds this morning."

"Happy shopping."

I was about to have some very happy shopping. I went to the vegetable department first, finding a ripe avocado, some fresh cilantro, a Roma tomato, some fresh garlic, and one small, sweet onion. I also found a shelf with egg roll wrappers — luckily, the coconut ones were in stock, so I got them.

Sparks were flying in my head as I gathered the rest of the ingredients for my Asian fusion-style egg roll recipe that I knew Jessa would love. A brilliant idea for a dipping sauce suddenly came to me. I grabbed one serrano pepper and one lime before going to pick up some lean steak from the meat department.

When I got to the meat department, I found one elderly lady taking her time as she moved from one section to another. She stood in the steak section, lingering for a while.

"Having trouble finding a good cut?" I asked as I looked over at the selection.

"Well, I've got these dentures, so it's hard to eat steak. But I love it so." She seemed daunted by the choices she had. "I'm just not sure what kind would be best for me."

"It's a little higher than most cuts, but the tenderness is well worth it." I pulled a filet mignon off the top shelf and showed it to her.

"Thirteen dollars! For one tiny steak?" she shook her head. "I'm not about to pay that for one steak."

"You'd pay up to fifty dollars for a steak like this in any steakhouse," I informed her. "It's not a bad price for this cut."

"And if I overcook it, or cook it wrong, then it'll be ruined," she argued.

"This cut is pretty hard to ruin. You can eat this rare or well done, and it'll still melt in your mouth." I pulled out my notepad, inside of which I'd written my notes for Jessa's meal. Jotting down the cooking directions for her, I pulled a twenty out of my wallet, then handed them both to her. "I'm paying for this one. And here's how to cook it. I wrote down the oven time for rare, medium, and well done, so you can pick which one you like best. Try it. It's on me."

She took the money and the note as she looked at me with curiosity in her pale green eyes. "Who are you?"

"Name's Stone Nash. I'm a chef." The pride I felt was insane. "You have a nice day, and enjoy that steak."

"I will. Thank you very much." Smiling as she walked away, I heard her humming happily.

Picking up a thin-cut sirloin, I had almost everything I needed for the egg rolls. Mexican crema and then some coconut oil were the only things I had left to make Jessa's meal.

I got the ingredients for the little snack bags too, making sure they were small enough to fit in the pockets of her scrubs. There would be no need for her to eat one single unhealthy thing throughout the entire day.

Checking out, the cashier yawned as she scanned the items. "Did you find everything okay, sir?"

"I did." I couldn't help but notice the bags under her eyes. She was tired, and that brought back to my mind the problem of being tired at work. There had to be foods that were good for you while helping you wake up and feel great. I looked at the various products shelved alongside the waiting line and found a bag of blueberries dipped in dark chocolate.

I handed them to her, and she ran them over the scanner. "You want these in a bag, or do you want them right now?" she asked.

"Don't put them in a bag. I bought them for you. I think they'll energize you and help you put the sleepiness behind you." I grabbed the bags she'd already filled with the rest of my items. "Next time I come in, which will probably be tomorrow morning, I'll ask if they've helped you or not. Okay?"

She looked at me like I was nuts. "Are you serious?"

"Very. If they do the trick, then I'm going to start making my own for the restaurant I'll be opening soon." I thought about the term restaurant — I wasn't sure that's what it would be. "Or café or shop or something along those lines. I haven't come up with the exact idea yet. But all the food will be delicious as well as healthy. I'll be using all sorts of superfoods."

She opened the package then popped one into her mouth. "My brother swears by this thing called hemp hearts. It's shelled hemp seeds, I think. He buys them here, he said, from the aisle with the flour and sugar and that kind of stuff. He says it tastes great, sort of nutty, but not too much. And he puts it on everything. He says it transforms any food into a superfood. You should get some."

"I'll have to check that out. Hemp hearts, right?" I knew speaking up about what I was aiming for would help me succeed faster than merely keeping everything to myself.

"Yeah, I'm pretty sure that's what it's called." She popped another chocolate-covered blueberry into her mouth. "I bet if you made these by hand, they'd taste even better. Like, the fresher the blueberry, the better it would taste."

"And perhaps being sprinkled with hemp hearts would make them taste better and be better for you." I loved the way my mind was working. "Thanks," I looked at her nametag, "Macie. I'm Stone. And I'm sure I'll be seeing lots more of you."

"Great." She ate another one, already looking much perkier. "See ya tomorrow."

Getting home around eight, I had to get to work on the foods. Just as I donned my apron, my brother Baldwyn called. I answered the call, "Hey, big bro. What's up?"

"Sloan wants to go try out something with you today. It's Greek cuisine. You up for it?"

"You bet I am." Greek food gave me the sudden idea of using grape leaves to wrap food up inside of it. "How about around one?"

"She's giving me the thumbs-up. She'll pick the place, then text it to you, and you guys can meet there."

My heart swelled as I felt all the love my family had for me. "Tell her I can't wait and thanks for doing this with me. I love you guys. And I think I've found something I'm crazy about too. I'll talk to her about it when I see her."

"What about talking about it with me?" he asked in a jealous tone.

"The next time we go to eat, I'll talk to you about it. I'd love to see your facial reaction when you hear my idea. I'll still need to try out foods from all over the world to incorporate them into my thing. I think it's going to be a whole new category. Maybe it can be called Texas fusion foods." I thought about how much it copied the Asian fusion thing and was quick to add, "Nope. Don't like it."

"I'm sure you'll come up with something great. I'm damn proud of you, baby bro."

Hearing someone say they were proud of me did things to my heart that felt great. "Aww, thanks, Baldwyn. See you later. And tell Sloan I'm excited."

"She is too. She's dying to hear your ideas. Bye."

"Bye." I ended the call, ready to get to work on Jessa's meal.

It was hard for me to remember what I'd done during the

days before finding my calling. I must've slept through them or something.

Now that I was wide awake and alert about what I wanted to do with my career, I was on fire. It took me no time at all to put together the egg rolls, then I let them rest in the fridge, wanting to freshen them just before taking them to her.

I had an hour or so leftover before I had to take off, so I took a little nap to help rejuvenate myself. There had never been a time in my life that I'd had so many thoughts running through my mind at the same time.

But the lack of sleep caught up to me and took me under its spell. Dreamless sleep pulled me in, enhancing my thoughts as I woke up without any hesitation when my alarm went off. "Time to get going."

## CHAPTER 16
## JESSA

Throughout the remainder of the night, I chastised myself over how quickly I had judged Stone based on the money he had. I didn't like to be judged, hence why I didn't talk freely about my family and worked to pay for my education anyway. I was actually hiding the fact that I came from a wealthy family while Stone just hadn't gotten around to telling me.

Stone had told me that I was scared — afraid to fall for anyone. I didn't like the idea of being afraid of anything. I was okay knowing that I might not know how to love a man, but being *afraid* to wasn't a thing that sat well with me.

I wasn't sure what I was going to do with that ill-feeling yet, but I did know that I wasn't going to actively push Stone away or try to find faults with him merely to justify why I didn't want to date him.

There was still the issue of my limited amount of time, but that was just the way things were. If he genuinely liked me, he'd keep on doing what he'd been doing, coming to see me at my jobs. If not, then at least I wouldn't have to blame myself for things not working out.

Sleep was a commodity that I couldn't live without. Being

upset with Stone had taken a toll on it, though. I'd barely gotten a couple of hours of rest, as I woke up many times wishing I hadn't said all the things I'd said to him. If I could've taken it all back, I would've.

My eyes were heavy as I walked into the hospital's cafeteria for my thirty-minute break. With how things had gone the night before, I had my doubts that Stone would actually come. My heart hung heavy in my chest, making it so that I couldn't pull my head up to see if he'd come or not.

*If he's not here, I might cry.*

"Morning," I heard his familiar voice saying.

Jerking my head up, I looked to my right. And there he sat, waiting for me at a small table for two. A black tray sat across from him. "Hi!" My heart leaped with excitement, hoping things between us would go back to normal. "You brought me something?"

"I said I would." He leaned back in his chair, stretching his long legs out to one side. "I worked on a recipe, then got up early this morning, got the ingredients, then went home and cooked. I got a wink or two in before I came up here. I feel rested, though. I think it's odd that I'm not exhausted. It must be from the excitement of finally having a project."

I took the empty seat, feeling a bit sheepish about how things had gone the night before. I needed to clear the air before I ate his food. "Stone, I'm really sorry about the things I said last night."

"I accept your apology. It's water under the bridge. So, take a gander at what I made for you." He leaned on his elbows, anticipating my reaction.

Pulling the lid off, I found three egg rolls, cooked to a perfect golden color. A slightly greenish sauce filled one of the side compartments. In the other side compartment was a small package of assorted nuts, berries, and other things. "So, we have egg rolls as the main course?" I asked, as those were usually side dishes.

"Yes, the egg rolls are the main course. I've named it the Tex-Mex egg rolls, and it comes with a serrano pepper-lime dipping sauce. And the little packet is full of protein-packed nuts and antioxidant berries. The dark chocolate chips are heart healthy. But the real kicker is the coconut flakes." He stopped to take a breath, as he was clearly excited.

"How are the coconut flakes the real kicker?" I couldn't wipe the smile off my face. He was just so excited about the food he'd prepared, and I found that adorable.

"They're also an antioxidant, but that's not all they are." He rubbed his hands together, almost resembling a scientist explaining something he finds extremely interesting.

I was getting a kick out of him. "Go on, Stone. Let me in on the secret."

"It's no secret. It's well documented and has been extensively researched. Coconut contains manganese. What this does is helps your body metabolize carbs, proteins, and cholesterol easier. So, eating a bit of coconut after any meal helps your digestive system work better. Plus, the manganese is good for your bones, and who doesn't need great bones?"

He'd been researching like a champ. "Stone, I've got to say that you seem to be on the way to being not only a great chef but an amazing nutritionist." I picked up one of the egg rolls and bit into it, finding it mildly spicy with flavors that burst to life inside my mouth. "Wow!"

His blue eyes lit up. "You like it?"

"I love it." There was such an array of wonderful tastes that it blew my mind. "Avocado?" I had to ask. "In an egg roll?"

"It works, though, right?" he asked.

"Creamily so." I couldn't get enough of it and took another bite. "The wrapper tastes a little different than what I'm used to. But I like it. There's a hint of…" I couldn't quite put my finger on it.

"Coconut," he offered. "The wrapper is made from

coconut flour. It makes it way healthier. And these were also deep fried in coconut oil. It might seem like a decadent treat, but it's really not. It's healthy in many ways."

Dipping it into the sauce, I took another bite and moaned with the amazing taste. "Yum!"

"I used store-bought Mexican crema, but I found a recipe for it, so I'm going to start making it myself. It's funny because I've always made my own crème fraiche. You can't find that in any regular grocery store anyway — I learned how to make it in culinary school. All you have to do to make Mexican crema is add the juice of one lime and some kosher salt to crème fraiche."

"You can make that stuff yourself?" I was impressed. "Stone, that's amazing. I thought those things were like cheese. You know — you need to have machines to make them or something like that."

"Nope. You can make them at home using nothing more than heavy whipping cream and buttermilk. It's a snap, really." The smile wouldn't leave his handsome face. "You can make your own cheese at home too, but you do need some special equipment for some of them. The soft cheeses are much easier to make on your own."

Seeing him so happy made me feel even worse for how I'd treated him the night before. "Stone, I really feel awful for the things I said yesterday."

"Yeah, you've apologized. We're good, Jessa." He acted as if the night before hadn't even happened. "I'm just so excited about this thing that I can't think of much else. I've got recipes floating through my mind as we speak. I've got ideas about the size of the place I want to open too. And I'm still working on what it should be called. A restaurant is too big for what I'm going for."

"What *are* you going for?" I wasn't sure I understood much about what he was planning."

"Okay, so I want to be able to make foods really quickly. I want things fresh. And I want there to be some places where people can sit down. But I don't want to waste time on hiring wait-staff. I want a walk-up type of thing where you walk up and see the menu on a board behind the counter. Maybe the specials will be written on a chalkboard at the door or in front of the cash register."

"I think you're talking about something along the lines of a bistro." I'd been to hundreds of them. "I like that atmosphere. Some soft music playing in the background, making everyone happy. I like instrumentals while I'm eating. The lights, not too bright, not too dim."

"Yeah." He reached out, taking my hands into his. "Help me, Jessa. Help me by telling me what is good and what's not. Help me with the ideas that would make this a place where lots of people would like to eat. I know you don't want my money, but I would love to pay you for consulting with me over this."

There was no way I could take his money. "I'll tell you what, Stone, you don't have to pay me in money since you're already feeding me. I think we're even. You give me free food — I give you my free opinion about it."

Cocking his head to one side, he seemed to be thinking about it. "For now."

"Sure, for now." It would be like that for as long as he needed my criticism of his food. But there wasn't any reason to argue over it. I was tired of arguing. I was tired of trying to fight whatever this thing between us was. I looked at the tray and realized that I'd devoured the food. All but the little packet. "Wow, I've finished." I held up the snack. "I'm going to keep this in my pocket to snack on throughout the day."

"Exactly what I wanted you to do with it." He was all smiles. "I'm going to look for biodegradable serving containers too. I want this thing to be as planet-friendly as it is good for people."

"I've got to tell you that I think you're doing something wonderful here." A sense of being on the edge of something big came over me. "I'm actually glad you've got money behind you to make this happen, Stone." If he hadn't had any, I would've definitely invested in his idea.

Shrugging, he looked a little modest. "I just hope I'm not reaching too far."

"You can't ever reach too far. Even if you only manage to grasp a part of your dream, more will come when it's time." I had some wise words for him, the same words that one of my first teachers in medical school had told our class. "Rome wasn't built in a day. But that doesn't mean Rome was unlivable the entire time it was being built. People still lived there when the construction was going on. Your business can still get going well before you're at the peak of this thing."

"You're saying that I should start small and not wait until I've hammered out every little detail, aren't you?"

"I *am* saying that." I had to get back to work. And for once, I was excited about going to see the babies in the nursery. At least, that little one who seemed to like only me. "I've gotta get going. And I'm off tonight, so I won't see you. But I'll be back here tomorrow if you care to come and see me. You don't always have to bring me food either."

"I know." He got up, taking the tray and throwing it away for me. "I *want* to bring you something to eat." He wrapped one arm around my shoulders, then pulled me to his side, his lips pressed against my temple. "I like the idea of you eating healthy."

"Well then, I look forward to eating what you come up with. Today's meal was off the charts delicious. And I don't feel the way I usually do when I leave this cafeteria or after I eat at Hamburger Hut. I feel great and not hungry in the least."

"I've got to figure out how to make this stuff at an affordable price, though. And that's gonna be the hardest part." Although faced with a daunting task, he still smiled.

As we got to where we had to part ways, I kissed his cheek. "See you tomorrow then, master chef."

Chuckling, he let me go. "See you tomorrow, future doctor."

I stood there for a moment, watching him walk away from me. *Nice butt. Why hadn't I noticed that before?*

## CHAPTER 17
## STONE

"It's sourdough," I told Jessa as I gave her the brown bag lunch, which I called the brown bag special.

"This is different from what you've been bringing me this past week." She sat down and opened it, pulling out the sandwich, chips, pickle, and a snack packet. Holding up the sandwich, she asked, "I thought bread wasn't good for you?"

"I found out that out of all the bread, sourdough is helpful to the body in ways that others aren't. It's full of prebiotics, which keeps your tummy happy. Plus, in most people, it doesn't cause blood sugar spikes. So, I went to the deli to find out what meat was on special. I bought it and a sliced cheese, which was also on special at the deli. I made homemade sweet potato chips, fried in coconut oil, and zested lightly with kosher salt. I added one of my homemade fermented pickles to spice things up and give added nutrition to the digestive system. And the snack packet that comes is made up of cheaper items, but they still pack some punch in the nutrition department. It has some coconut flakes and some type of chip, albeit chocolate, vanilla, or even butterscotch, peanuts for the main nut, and a few pecans and cashews. You get plenty of nutrition for a little money with the brown bag special."

"You haven't sat down," she pointed out.

I didn't want to disappoint her, but the fact was that I was getting pretty busy with this thing. "I've gotta get to the resort to meet with my brother Cohen. He's found some information on getting some grants."

Holding up a finger, she swallowed the bite of the sandwich she'd taken. "First, this is the most amazing sandwich I've ever had the good fortune to taste. When my lips felt the room temperature bread, I didn't expect warm meat and melty cheese."

"I put the meat and cheese on a tray, keeping them in individual piles, then heated them until the cheese melted a bit. I didn't heat the entire sandwich, so the bread could remain soft, and the mayonnaise doesn't get warm. Plus, you can add the fresh veggies without them getting wilted." I knew that techniques like that would make my food stand out in the crowd.

"This is mayonnaise?" She looked at me with narrowed, disbelieving eyes.

"I made it myself." I'd found that I could make most condiments for less money than buying them in bulk. Plus, they all tasted better. "You've got to keep in mind that this is for the special. It's not the same as the premium mayo that I make for other things. In this one, I mix a cheaper olive oil with the egg whites. Since the special at the deli was roast beef, I used balsamic vinegar as the acid to enhance the flavor. You like it?"

"I love it. I could eat this mayo alone." She took another bite — a dollop of the creamy white stuff dropping on her chin.

Grabbing a napkin, I quickly wiped it off. "Lost some."

Her cheeks went pink as she ducked her head. "Thanks for getting it for me. And since you have plenty of money to make this happen, why are you looking at trying to get grants?"

"Well, I've got an idea in mind that would benefit some people if I could get a grant. As my brothers have taught me, you can't give things away all the time. You have to watch that bottom line. So, I'm trying to find a way to do some giving while still making something for my bistro."

"Ah, you've decided to call it a bistro then?" she asked with a sly smile.

"Maybe. I'm still kicking things around. But I like the way you said the word. It's sort of stuck in my head now."

"Glad I got something stuck in there." Picking up the pickle, she looked at it reluctantly. "You called this a fermented pickle, right?"

"All that means is that I brined it in a saltwater solution instead of vinegar. And it can't be stored on a shelf. It must be stored in the fridge after it's set out a number of days to get the fermentation process started. In the fridge, the pickles continue to ferment, but at a much slower rate." I knew I had to get going but hated to leave her. We had so little time together as it was, and now that things seemed to be about to ramp up, I felt uneasy about our future. "It's much better for you than any other pickle. You know, gut-friendly." I leaned in, kissing her cheek. "Baby, I've gotta jet. I've got a million things to do. If I'm scarce for the next bit, it's not because of you — it's work. But shoot me a text now and then, and I'll shoot them back to you as soon as I get a chance."

A crease in her brow had me a little worried until she said, "I like seeing you this driven, Stone — I really do. Keep following that passion, and you're sure to make something spectacular. You know where I'll be. I'm not going anywhere. But does this mean I'm gonna miss out on your great lunches?"

I felt awful. "Yeah, for a while. I've gotta get things rolling. Time is a real witch, isn't it?"

"It sure is." She reached up, pulling me back to her, leaving a kiss on my cheek. "I'll text you to let you know I haven't forgotten about you."

"And I'll do the same."

Hurrying off to meet with Cohen, it dawned on me that I

hadn't ever felt this way. It was like I had a real purpose. He was at his desk when I entered his office. "I'm late, I know. I had to stop by the hospital to give Jessa something. But I've told her that I will no longer have time to do that. So, let's see what you've found."

"You know, I'm glad you're making this a priority, Stone. But keep the girl in the loop. Don't lose her over this." He pulled up a website on his computer. "Anyway, sage advice over. Here's the deal on the grants. There are some that help feed different kinds of people. Students mostly."

"Can't interns be called students?" I thought that was essentially what they were. "They get paid damn little, I'd expect."

"You mean to tell me that you're seeing an intern, and you haven't asked her how they get paid?" He shook his head. "Well, thanks to me, you won't need to ask her that. Interns who work at hospitals are paid by the Department of Health and Human Services. What they make is low enough to make them eligible for some of these grants that I've found."

I slapped him on the back, my body heating with excitement. "Fantastic! We're gonna make this happen!"

"We can make it happen. But the only thing in the way right now is that you don't have an established restaurant or other food service businesses. So you, my little brother, need to make up your mind about several things here. The menu. The venue. And then you've got a whole lot of other things you have to decide upon."

*Crap, that's a fuck-lot of work.*

"How long do I have to be open to have an established business?" I felt time slipping away from me like sands through an hourglass. And it was not fun at all.

"Six months. After that, you can apply for the grants, and then that'll take more time. But, in the meantime, I've got a great idea."

"And the great idea is?" There had to be something we could do to make things go faster.

"If you can get all our brothers and our cousins to agree, we can make up a grant of our own that will cover you until you can get something from the federal government to keep you going."

I couldn't help it. I grabbed him by the face then smacked him dead on the lips. "Thank you!" I turned to leave, nearly running, as I knew right where I wanted to set up my very first bistro. "You're the smartest man ever! I'll secure the place then our family." I kicked up my heels. "Woo! Hoo!"

"Yee-haw," Cohen shouted. "Go get 'em, tiger."

Everything was coming like a flash of lightning. I knew it meant I was on the right path. I returned to the hospital Jessa interned at and went up to the lady standing behind the front desk. "How can I help you today, sir?"

"Who would I need to talk to about opening a small bistro in this hospital?"

"That would be Evelyn Dowdy, the food service department administrator." She slid a business card across the desk. "You can reach her at this number."

I knew it would be a hell of a long shot that she'd be able to see me today, but I walked away to a nearby empty waiting room and made the call.

She picked up on the first ring, "Evelyn Dowdy."

"Hi, Ms. Dowdy. This is Stone Nash. I'd like to see if I can get a meeting with you about a bistro I'd like to open in your hospital."

"I'm in my office right now. I'm about to leave in an hour, but I'll be gone for two weeks on vacation. Can you make it within the hour?"

I began walking toward the elevators. "I'm here now. What room number is yours?"

"Top floor, room eight-zero-one."

"Be there in a couple of minutes." I got onto the elevator,

nervous as hell as I went up to find out whether this would be the place where I would begin this adventure.

Knocking on her slightly ajar office door, I heard her pleasant voice as she said, "Come in, Stone Nash."

"Thanks for seeing me on such short notice." I took the seat across from her as she sat at the desk.

"You said you'd like to open a bistro here?"

"It'll be a bit more than that. See, I'm going to be applying for grants to feed the interns for free. I'm only going to be serving healthy foods. I'll sell to others, but the interns will each get a free meal every day."

"That sounds amazing. But I know that grants don't happen overnight." She turned around the laptop she had in front of her, showing me that she'd pulled up my name on a search engine. "I see you aren't lacking in money. But I've got to wonder why you would want to open something here instead of at that amazing resort you and your brothers own."

"I've seen a need for what I'm specializing in, and the need is within hospitals. I'll eventually put a bistro in every hospital that'll accept me. But I'd like to start this right here."

"I've got space available. But there's a lot you'll have to do." She took out a pen and a piece of paper from her desk drawer. "I'll write it down for you. We'll need the menu that you plan to serve. And the prices you'll be charging. The number of employees, too. And you should know that anyone who works within these walls must pass an aggressive background check."

"I understand that." It sounded like a lot of work was ahead of me, but I was up for it.

"We'll also need a strategic business plan. I can't tell you the rent until we deem you acceptable as a vendor. But I can tell you that it's not cheap. You still in?"

"I'm in." A thought popped into my head. "Do you think it would be possible to leave some food samples somewhere around here so I can get some feedback?"

"The nurse's stations always appreciate free food. And the doctor's lounge is a good place for those sorts of things too." She pulled out another pad and scribbled something on it before sliding it to me. "You'll give this to whoever is working the front desk. Watch to make sure she keys everything into the computer. Then wait until she gives you a badge — it will allow you to come and go, even after hours when the doors are locked."

"Wow." This young lady was really helping me. "I can't thank you enough."

"Hey," she said as she looked at me with kind eyes. "I think what you want to do is amazing. I'm rooting for you, Stone Nash. And I'll do everything I can to help you make this work. But for the next two weeks, I'll be out of the office and out of town. My boyfriend and I are heading to Cancun. But please, come see me the day I get back. I'll be dying to know all you've achieved in that time."

*This is really going to happen!*

# CHAPTER 18
## JESSA

**-Wanted to say hi. I see now what you were saying about how something you feel passionate about can take up almost all of your time. I've only got time to catch a few hours of sleep, and my mind keeps going even then. Miss you. Thinking about you. -**

Midnight had just rolled around, and I was writing a financial report at Hamburger Hut. It had only been three days since I'd last seen Stone. The day he'd brought me the brown bag special that was unlike any special I'd ever had.

**-Miss you too. Proud of you, though. One day, you'll be able to slow down a bit, catch your breath. When you do, I hope I'm at a slow moment in my life too. Absence makes the heart grow fonder, someone once said. I'm here to say that it's true. I've grown quite fond of you, Stone. Night. -**

It wasn't easy to get Stone off my mind as I added and subtracted numbers for the report. Once my shift was over, I went home, feeling a little lonely. I hadn't even realized that I'd gotten used to Stone's company, even if it hadn't been more than bits of stolen minutes here and there. I missed seeing his face and hearing his voice.

He must've been swamped if he hadn't had time to call in the last three days. Even though it was on a much smaller scale than an entire restaurant, opening a bistro must be hard and time-consuming work.

The next morning, I'd packed a turkey sandwich and a bag of chips for lunch and grabbed it on my way out. Getting to the hospital, I'd hid the bag way in the back of the fridge, hoping no one would find it. I'd written my name on it too, but that would mean nothing to a starving nurse or intern or even a doctor.

When I walked past the nurse's station in the emergency department, I smelled something with cinnamon. Looking around, I found a tray of small golden cubes. "These for anybody?" I asked the closest nurse.

"Yeah. You have to take and fill out a card, then leave it in that little box. Or you could do it online too." She pointed them out, and I took a card before taking a sample.

The nurse took a sample too. "It's my third one, but I can't help myself. They're so good."

Taking a nibble, I wasn't sure what I was eating — I tasted egg, ham, and something sort of nutty and cheesy. "Wow, like a full breakfast in one bite."

"Yeah, breakfast bites," she said, then pulled out a card she had in her pocket and wrote something down on it. "One of the questions is about product names. I think breakfast bites fits."

"I agree." I popped the whole thing into my mouth as I looked at the card. The ingredients were on the back of the card, together with the nutrition statistics. There were a few questions on the front of the card. One of them was what names you would give to this food. Another one was about appearance. And then there was one about the taste rating on a one to ten scale. "I'd rate this an eight."

"I'd give it a ten," the nurse countered. "It's got it all in one bite. I'd say maybe five or six of these things, and you've got an entire meal out of the way."

The web address was vague, too — answerfoodques-tionshere.com.

"Do you have any idea who brought these?" I had to wonder if Stone had something to do with it. The food was great. The nutrition stats had him written all over them too.

"Not a clue. I'm thinking it must be some food company that wants to see if these are good enough to package and sell, probably in the frozen food section." She looked around as the door to the ER opened. "Duty calls."

"See ya." I went down the hallway then took a left to see if I could find a doctor to shadow for the first part of my day. No one was around the emergency department, so I headed to the ICU and found some more food there. "Hey," I said to the intern snacking on something. "What have you got there?"

"Well, it's ham rolled around some cheesy tasting eggs. But the egg is flat, so they roll up great together. And there's some other stuff in the egg, like bell peppers and stuff like that. It's good. One was pretty much good enough to fill me, but they taste so good that I'm on my second one."

More little business cards sat next to the tray. I picked up a card and a ham roll, reading the ingredients. "It says there are hemp hearts in this." I had no idea what those were. "You feeling okay after eating two of these?"

"Are you serious right now?" he laughed. "That stuff can't get you high. Not even a little. Do you know anything about pot, Miss Moxon?"

"No, not really." Real pharmaceuticals classes didn't hand out any information on marijuana. I took a bite and found it good even though it was at room temperature. "Yum."

I took out my pen and jotted down breakfast rolls where it asked for a name for the product. I knew it was a spin-off from the breakfast bite, but I didn't care.

Another intern walked up with something in her hand.

"Hey, I found these in the maternity ward. Check it out." She opened the lid of a Styrofoam container. "It's a freaking Monte Cristo sandwich. Only it's got lots more stuff in it. Red, yellow, and green bell peppers are mixed in with the scrambled egg. And it tastes like there's cheese in it, but there ain't any. It's something called nutritional yeast." She held out one of the small cards. "Look at the ingredients."

"Sourdough bread." I stopped and looked up as I remembered that Stone had used sourdough bread in the last thing he'd made for me. "Interesting. Smoked ham, farm-fresh eggs mixed with a variety of bell peppers, and nutritional yeast to replace cheese." I noticed there was kosher salt on the list too. I knew that was something Stone used exclusively over regular salt. "Did either of you see who delivered these trays?"

They both shook their heads. I popped the rest of the breakfast roll into my mouth before setting off to check out each department's nurse's stations for healthy foods.

I found most of the trays empty by the time I got to them all. And no one had seen the person who'd delivered these things either. So, since I had the night off from Hamburger Hut, I got on the computer as soon as I got home.

Pulling the business card out of my pocket, I punched in the web address, confident that it would give me more insight into who was behind this. I'd been wrong. The page was in black and white and offered nothing about who or what company was behind the free samples.

I filled out the questionnaire anyway, leaving my genuine reviews of the foods I'd had a chance to try. Right before I hit the submit button, I had the oddest feeling that I might be helping out what could become a rival of Stone. So, I deleted everything.

I couldn't send such great feedback to someone who was Stone's rival. He was so enthralled with this endeavor. He spent every waking moment on it. I couldn't go behind his back and give kudos to anyone else. I was his cheerleader and would not cheer for any other teams.

Putting that out of my mind, I checked my classes and found some pleasant surprises. We only had three essay questions for one class and four multiple-choice tests for another. There was reading to do for the last class, and I knew I could do that while working nights.

I had time for an actual shower. I had time to eat something, too, and thought about ordering take-out. After a nice long shower, I dressed in some comfy sweats, then went to check out the many menus I'd collected from the restaurants near me that delivered.

Nothing looked as good as the things Stone had been making for me, though. Nothing seemed healthy in the least either. Salad after salad was all anyone offered that was on the healthy side. But I didn't want a lousy salad. I wanted something substantial. I wanted something that would leave me feeling great — the way Stone's food did.

Looking at my cell sitting on the coffee table, I thought about doing it — calling Stone. He was most likely very busy with things. But still, I wondered where he was working.

The night's work wouldn't be that strenuous on me. I could talk to him a little while doing the majority of it. I missed talking to him. I missed seeing him. Those soft kisses to my cheek were things I missed too.

Closing my eyes, I moved my feet, tucking them underneath me as I settled on the sofa. I imagined his face, his muscular body, his lips that were thick yet somehow chiseled, as if someone had carved them out of marble. And then there were those eyes, deep-set, blue as the Pacific Ocean, and playful, dancing ever so often when he talked.

Stone's playful spirit was only rivaled by his passionate one. And if he could be that passionate about opening a restaurant, he could be equally passionate about love or making love.

Warmth blossomed inside of me. I lay my head back on

the sofa, moaning as I thought about his lips pressing against mine. His hands caressing my skin as he ran them over every last inch of me. His body moving over mine, his weight not only bearable but desired. To feel him that way would be an experience I would never forget.

Opening my eyes, I knew that was a pipedream. At least for now.

*Maybe one day we'll both have some time to see where things might lead.*

"Hi, Ember. I've got tomorrow's trays ready. Do you want me to send them over now?" I'd enlisted the help of my sister-in-law and niece, Madison, to get the food samples to the hospital. Doing all the recipe development, shopping, cooking, and keeping an eye on the reviews left me with little time to get the food to where it needed to be.

"Yeah, send them over. We're home. Madison is loving this job too. She's so happy that you're letting her do this," Ember said. "You might laugh at this, but she said she would've done it for the food alone. She's loved everything you've made so far."

"I wasn't about to ask you guys to do all of this for free. I figure you two should be on my payroll anyway since I'm sure that I'll need both your help when I get this thing open." I wasn't about to let great help escape me.

Ember's laugh made me smile. "We're family, Stone. We would've helped even if we had to do it for free. But I have to say that I like the fact that Madison is already beginning to learn what it means to actually earn money, and how to save it, and when she does spend it, to do it wisely. I know none of us are hurting for money, but it never hurts to know its value."

"I agree." I thought about how mad Jessa had gotten after finding out that I'd neglected to tell her about the wealth I had and her reasons behind that anger. "If we'd been born into this kind of money, I don't know if we'd have become the same hardworking people we are today. I'm glad I can help teach Madison to respect money and respect people who work hard for it."

"I'm glad you're able to help with this lesson as well, Stone. I'll talk to you tomorrow then. Bye, now."

"Bye, Ember. Tell Cohen hi for me." I ended that call, then used the app to get an Uber to deliver the food to Ember.

As soon as I put the phone down, it lit up, and I saw I had a message from Jessa. My heart skipped a beat, and a smile immediately formed on my lips. "Wonder what she's doing tonight." I was sure she was very busy, as always. But one could hope for a change in her usual schedule.

Swiping the screen, I read her text.

**- Just sitting at home, thinking of you. How's your night going? -**

I wasn't going to let a phone call go by while she was just sitting around, so I called her, and she picked up on the first ring. "Hey, you."

"I see you've been missing me," I teased her.

"I think I wrote that I was thinking of you, not missing you," she said with light laughter.

The sound tickled my ear. "I read between the lines and found more to it than just that. What has you being able to just sit around this evening?"

"My assignments aren't as intense as they normally are, so I've got a little bit more downtime. What are you up to?"

"How much more downtime do you have left?" A spark of hope lit up inside of me.

"Well, I do have some work to do, but it shouldn't take me more than two hours. Then I'll have the rest of the night free. Of course, I still have to get up early to get to the hospital tomorrow. Maybe we can talk a little on the phone tonight."

"Maybe you can come over, and I'll make you dinner." I wasn't about to waste our mutual free time talking on the phone. "I'll send a car to pick you up, and you can bring your laptop to continue working while you're heading my way. And I'll get one to take you home later too. How does that sound?"

She didn't say anything for a moment, then said, "Okay."

I actually felt my heart pounding in my chest. "Great. Our first real date. I'm gonna make it special, too."

"Stone, don't go out of your way for me. I'm just glad to hang out with you for a while. Promise me that you'll keep it simple."

"Sure, I'll keep it simple." I wasn't about to keep it simple. I wanted to show her how great it could be if she gave me more of her precious time. "I'll text you when the car's there. And just so you know, I cannot wait."

"Me too. See you soon."

Closing the computer, I grabbed it and went to put it away before I began rushing around, trying to turn the small dining area into the most romantic setting possible.

There were filet mignons in the fridge that I'd begun thawing out the day before for a special type of egg roll I was planning to make the following afternoon. But now I would use a couple of them for us.

I popped into the kitchen, pulling the filets out of the fridge and sitting them on the cutting board to let them reach room temperature. Grabbing a couple of potatoes, I turned on the oven to preheat it before wrapping them in foil. I could put a salad together just before we sat down to eat.

I enjoyed throwing little intimate dinners. I'd done it for all my brothers and the women they eventually married. And I'd done it for many of my friends too. But this was the first time I was doing it for myself.

And since I was doing this for Jessa and me on our first real date, nerves began forming inside me like thunderheads, and I completely lost track of things.

Standing there in the middle of my kitchen, I shouted, "I forgot to get a car on its way to her!"

Reaching into my back pocket, I didn't find my phone there and felt panic rising. Jerking my head towards the last place I'd been with my phone, I found it sitting on the bar.

Taking deep breaths to ease the stress, I froze, as I hadn't even asked for Jessa's address. My finger hovered over my contacts list so that I could call her to get the address when a text came in. She'd texted it to me, and I sighed with relief. "Damn, I'm losing it."

After getting a car headed to Jessa's and setting it up to pick up the bags of food I had to take to Ember afterwards, I went back to work on the dining room. Stringing some twinkling white lights along one side of the room, I created a starry night effect. A white linen tablecloth and my go-to centerpiece in a pinch — a clear glass, wide mouth vase filled with polished river rocks and a fat white candle buried three inches into them — made the table look as elegant as one in any five-star restaurant.

Stepping back, I admired my work before using my phone to connect to the hidden Bluetooth speakers and put on some soft, instrumental music. I remembered Jessa saying that she liked listening to that kind of music while eating.

With the mishap of waiting to get a car to Jessa, I'd gained about twenty minutes until she would arrive, so I got out all the fresh veggies I had and began preparing our salads. A fair amount of nerves were still bothering me, so I pulled a couple of bottles of red wine out of the wine cooler and opened them so they could breathe a bit.

To fix my nerve problem, I also got out a bottle of Jack Daniels and poured myself a shot. "Down the hatch." I tossed it back, swallowing the hot liquor. "Damn, that's good."

As I peeled and chopped the ingredients for the salad, I

wondered if Jessa was feeling the same way I was. We'd never been alone together. We'd always had others around us, and we were always in public as well. This was new, unusual for both of us. I just hoped our nerves wouldn't make for an awkward evening.

I gave myself one more shot before putting the whisky bottle back into the cabinet. The edge would soon be gone, and I could be the man I really was, not this bundle of nerves I'd never been in my life.

As I poured myself into cooking, I began figuring out why all the nerves had come up in the first place. The thing was that I wasn't sure how I was supposed to act.

I couldn't be the man I was with every other woman. I couldn't be flirty and have the usual one goal — to get into her pants. I had to be better than that — somehow.

We might not have spent much time together, but it felt like I'd spent more time with her than I'd spent with any other woman. Maybe it was because we'd spent our time talking and not grinding on one another.

Those little kisses we'd left on each other's cheeks were the only intimacy we'd shared. But the thing about those little kisses was that I remembered each and every one of them. I remembered how warm her skin had been when I kissed her the very first time. And she'd smelled like lemon floor cleaner for some reason. But I liked it.

When her lips had touched my cheek that first time, I had actually blushed. And my legs had felt like noodles — only for a split second, but they'd gone weak for her.

Jessa wasn't just some girl. For all I knew, she might be *the* girl. There was no way I would try to rush to debating whether she was the one for me or not. We both had loads of things we wanted to accomplish before getting into something that concrete.

Just knowing that those little kisses meant more to me than any kiss I'd ever gotten or given was enough to tell me that

Jessa Moxon was someone special to me. And I needed to treat her that way too.

Assembling the salad, I put in extra effort, because wanted it to be gorgeous for her. I wanted everything to be perfect for our first date. She might not have known it about herself, but I thought she was a perfect woman.

Jessa knew what she wanted and wouldn't let anything get in her way of becoming a doctor. I had no idea what kind of money her family had, but they obviously didn't have the kind of money to help their daughter pay for all the classes she had to take. She did that on her own.

That alone was something deserving of respect, something no one could ever take away from her. She'd worked her ass off for what she wanted. And the amazing thing about that was that she wanted to help other people. She wanted to make people feel better. And for that, she was willing to give up her social life to work a shitty job.

I placed the salads in the fridge, leaned back against the stainless-steel doors, and closed my eyes. It occurred to me that I was afraid of not being able to live up to what she deserved. She deserved a real man. She deserved to have someone to come home to, someone who could take all the hardships of her busy and probably emotionally straining days away with one kiss, one hug, and a whole lotta love.

I shivered as fear ran like ice through my veins. My parents had died when I was only eight years old. Not having them around as role models for how marriages go was an issue. I wasn't sure how to treat a woman who I respected but wanted to have sex with.

*I can't screw this up.*

# CHAPTER 20
## JESSA

The driver pulled through the open gates, slowly proceeding up the long driveway. Stone's mansion stood three stories high, yet it looked right at home, nestled into the surrounding hills. Spotlights pointed out various foliage adorning the nooks and crannies of the front side of the house. Double wooden doors pulled open, and Stone stood there, barefoot in blue jeans and a white button-down shirt left untucked. He looked relaxed and happy to see me.

My body warmed as I watched him coming out to greet me. He opened the door for me, and only then did I see the large black bag in his hand. "Hi."

His eyes sparkled. "Hi." He placed the bag in the backseat I'd just vacated. "Here you go. You've got the address and the number to text once you're there. Someone will come out and pick it up. Thanks."

"Sure thing, Mr. Nash."

Stone ran his arm around my waist, pulling me close. "It's good to see you."

"You too." I gazed at the home that didn't seem nearly as stoic as the turn of the century mansion I called home. "Nice place you've got here."

"I call it home. Don't let the size of this place get to you. It's big and full of nice things, but this is my home, not some museum. I want you to make yourself at home and get nice and comfy."

Walking into the foyer, I looked up and saw that it went all the way to the very top of the third floor. "Nice feature."

"Thanks." He closed the doors behind us, then tapped on a keypad on the wall. "Gotta close the gates behind the Uber. Otherwise, the neighbor's dogs will come and crap in my yard."

"Sweet." I laughed.

His hand slipped into mine as he led me through a large living area with a gorgeous, lit-up fireplace, the flames dancing invitingly. "This is the living room. I rarely spend time here. It's just too big for me, alone, to feel comfortable in. I wanted you to see the fireplace lit, though. It's one of my favorite things about this house."

"It's beautiful. I can imagine sleeping in front of it on that cowskin rug you've got there." Romance seemed to be filling the air, and for once, I wasn't trying to find a way out of it.

His deep chuckle stirred me in ways that I found quite pleasurable. "Maybe later, hun."

Moving on, he took me through a short hallway, and then we were in the kitchen. "This is where I feel most at home." He put his hands on my waist, lifting me to sit on a tall barstool. "Take that laptop out of the bag you've got hanging on your shoulder. You can get to that classwork of yours while I get to cooking our steaks."

"Steaks?" I liked the sound of that. "And what else do you have going on for tonight's dinner?" I pulled the laptop out of my bag, placing it on the bar but not opening it.

"You said to keep it simple, so I did." He pulled out a couple of aluminum foil-wrapped objects from the oven. "Baked potatoes and salad. There's red wine chilling too." He filled one of the two wine glasses that sat next to an ice bucket with two uncorked bottles inside. "Here you go. This will help you settle in."

As I sipped on mine, he filled one for himself too. "This is divine, Stone."

Putting an iron skillet on the stovetop, he pulled a cutting board towards him, on which were laying the two steaks. "Filet mignon. Sounds okay to you, baby?"

"Sounds perfect." I had to hand it to the man. He sure knew how to treat a lady. "You're spoiling me."

"I don't think a woman as wonderful as you can be spoiled." He poured a bit of oil into the skillet.

"What kind of oil is that?" I ignored my computer, as Stone captivated me by how he moved with such grace as he cooked.

"Grapeseed oil. I use it when I'm cooking steaks or chicken. It's got a higher burning point than olive oil, so it can really sear steak and chicken well. Searing the meat keeps the juices locked inside as they should be."

The seasonings were sitting on the butcher's block countertop. "I see you've prepared for this."

"Of course." He used his fingers to pick up some salt, and then held his hand up high to sprinkle it over the two cuts of meat.

"Kosher?"

"I use nothing else."

The bag he'd left with the driver suddenly came back to mind as I recalled the food samples I'd eaten at the hospital. "Stone, where are you sending that bag you left with the driver? And what was in it?"

His lips pulled up only halfway as he cocked one brow. "I've got some exciting news. I'm going to open my first bistro in the hospital you're working in."

"The bag had trays of food in it, didn't it?" I knew it did.

"Yes, it did. I sent it to my brother Cohen's house. His wife, Ember, and their daughter, Madison, have been taking it to the hospital early each morning to put it out at the nurse's stations and the doctor's lounge. I've been getting their feedback, and so far, it's mostly been great. My menu is just about complete."

"I had a feeling that it was your food." I couldn't wipe the smile off my face. "I was about to leave my review on the website, but I got worried that it might not be you, and I might be giving your competitor more praise than I should."

"It's me. I've been working day and night on recipes, and it's been nice having people giving me ideas of what to call everything. You don't have to go to the website. You can just tell me what you think." He leaned over the bar, running his fingers over the back of my hand. "I think it's cool that you knew it was my food just by tasting it. We've got a rather good connection, you and I."

Ducking my head, I wore a shy smile. "You think?"

"I do." He dropped the fillets into the hot pan, where they sizzled loudly. "Two minutes on each side, including all the way around their sides, and then I'll pop them into the oven for ten minutes. Unless you want yours well done."

"I'll take it the way you like to cook it. I trust your judgment." I was beginning to trust him more than I'd ever trusted anyone. "I've said I was sorry for the things I said to you, but I really am. I mean, I'd pegged you as a bratty rich guy, and that was extremely wrong of me. You're not bratty or spoiled in the least. I can't stop kicking myself for even thinking that or saying a thing to you about it."

"Just stop kicking yourself already. I'm fine. I'm not used to people not automatically knowing that I've got money now. Ever since we came to Austin from Houston, where we grew up, everyone around this city has known us as the rich guys who built a resort. I just assumed you knew who I was when I told you my name. And if you didn't know at that exact moment, people usually Google someone they've just met and get the scoop on them."

"Guess I was a little too busy to do any Goggling. At least

not until one of the doctors at the hospital told me about you being a billionaire who was on the cover of Texas Monthly." I still felt ashamed of myself for judging Stone so harshly. "If I could take that back, I certainly would."

"I know you would." He topped off the wine in my glass. "Have as much as you want. I'm having a driver come to take you home too."

Sipping on the wine, I felt taken care of. Most of the times that I'd begun to feel that way with a man, I would find myself easing away from him. I didn't want to be taken care of. But the way Stone was doing it didn't bother me at all. "Thanks. I will enjoy myself with you this evening."

He glanced at my unopened computer. "How much work do you have to get done?"

"I've got about another hour to go." I didn't want to get to the work at all. I wanted to sit there, talking to Stone, sipping at the wine, and feeling like someone who didn't work an eighty-hour week. "I'll do it after we eat. I'm actually loving watching you cook."

"Then please, keep watching." He used the tongs expertly to turn the meat until both pieces were evenly seared. "Gorgeous, huh?"

He was talking about the color of the meat, but I was talking about him. "Yes, gorgeous." I took another sip, licking the slightly salty drink off my lips. "I'm glad I had time to shower before I came over. It's been a while since I groomed myself. Glad I took the time to clean myself up for tonight."

"You look lovely. But you always look lovely to me." Pulling the skillet off the stovetop, he popped it into the oven built into the wall. "Can I tell you something?" He leaned on the bar in front of me, his fingers intertwined as he looked into my eyes.

"I suppose so." My stomach stirred a little as I became nervous that he was going to ask me about myself — like what kind of family I came from or something. And I did not want to tell him about that aspect of myself at all.

"I remember each kiss on the cheek that you gave me, and I gave you. I remember the way your skin felt on my lips. I remember the way you smelled."

"Oh, no." I blushed. "God, Stone, I must've smelled awful all those times. If it wasn't hamburger grease, it was probably floor cleaner. That hospital always reeks of it." I was glad I'd spritzed myself with a little sweetly scented body spray. At least his memory of my smell on our first date wouldn't horrify me.

"It was lemon scent, and I adored it."

"Floor cleaner," I muttered, then took another drink. "And you always smell like a million bucks. *Always.*"

"Thanks, babe." He turned and went to the fridge, then returned with a stick of butter. "For the steaks. Once they've cooked, I slather butter on top of them. It makes them even juicer, and when you cut into the meat, releasing the juices, they mix with the butter, making the best dipping sauce. I hate steak sauce. Won't even serve it."

"That's because you're a true chef. And I am proud that I know you, Chef Nash." I held up my wine glass. "Cheers to you."

"Nah." He waved his hand in front of his face as if I'd embarrassed him. "I've never liked being called Chef Nash. It sounds pretentious."

"It's an honor to be called something like that, Stone. You're wonderful at what you do. Accept the title you've earned." I held my glass up again. "Here's to Chef Nash, the best cook in the entire world."

"You're biased because I've fed you for free." He laughed as he turned away from me to get the steaks out of the oven.

He was right. I was biased. But not because he'd fed me for free. I thought it had more to do with how much I'd begun to adore him.

# CHAPTER 21
## STONE

After dinner, I cleaned up the kitchen while Jessa completed her classwork. Music played softly as we finished up the day's work. Just as I started the dishwasher, she closed her laptop. "Done."

I'd never heard such a beautiful word in my life. "Me too."

Moving toward her, she smiled as I turned the barstool she was sitting on around until she was facing me. Her hands moved over my cheeks as she gazed into my eyes. "I think I should kiss the cook for the fine meal he made and the ultra-romantic setting he put together. What do you think?"

"I think that's the best idea I've ever heard in my entire life." It felt as if I'd been waiting an eternity for this moment.

She pulled me to her, and our lips barely grazed, sending zaps of electricity shooting throughout my entire body. I couldn't help myself from doing what I did next, scooping her up in my arms as the kiss took on a life of its own.

Her thumb moved back and forth along my jawline while she ran the other hand around my neck, hanging on to me. Carrying her to the sofa in the adjoining room, I sat down, putting her on my lap. The weight of her body on mine took me under.

Before I knew it, she was on her back, and I was all over her, both of us touching and exploring everything we could with our clothes still on. It may have seemed too fast, but it wasn't like I could stop it.

I held her tightly to me then rolled off the sofa, landing on my back on the carpeted floor. Rolling over, Jessa was underneath me again. Our mouths wouldn't part, and the kiss wouldn't end. My hands had a mind of their own as they began pulling her clothes away from her body, eager to touch flesh instead of material.

Her hands worked hard, too, unbuttoning my shirt then pulling it off. Moaning, she ran her hands over my back, arching so I could rid her of her pants. While I was at it, I removed mine too. And somehow, our lips still hadn't parted.

The way my skin felt as it moved against hers wasn't human in any way. The softest silk couldn't compare to hers. I wanted to feel every last part of her. I *had* to feel her. I *needed* to feel her more than I'd ever needed anything. I would've given up the air in my lungs just to get to touch every last inch of her.

She moved one hand, wrapping it around my cock. The sound I let out was more animal than human, and the kiss went to an even deeper place. Stroking me with perfect rhythm, she brought my erection to the fullest it had ever been. And then, she spread her legs, guiding me to where she wanted me.

Knees bent, she arched to meet me, urging me inside as our kiss became much softer, much sweeter. I slid my hands over her shoulders as I entered her, feeling the tightness, the slickness, and the tenderness of her womanhood.

*I could live right here, inside of her, forever.*

We moved together like we'd done this a thousand times before, knowing what the other was going to do before they even did it. I pulled my lips away from hers so I could look into her eyes. What I found hit me right in the heart. "I've never seen love in anyone's eyes before yours."

She gulped as one tear slipped down her cheek. "Does that scare you?"

"Not even a little." I kissed the tip of her nose as our bodies swayed to music only we could hear. I pulled back, looking into her eyes again. "What do you see in mine?"

Closing her eyes, she smiled before opening them again. "It's still there. I wasn't sure whether what I was seeing was real or not. But it's still there. You sort of have a crush on me, don't you?" she joked.

"I might have a small one, yeah." I ran my fingers along her arm then lifted it, kissing a line down along it. "I just want you to know that I wasn't even thinking that this was how our night would end."

"You weren't trying to seduce me with your delicious food, the romantic twinkling lights, and the wine?" Her nails lightly raked across my back.

"Not at all." I'd wanted us to have a romantic night, but sex hadn't been anywhere on my radar. "But if that's what it takes to get to this, then I'll do it every damn night."

"You don't think you'll get tired of me?"

Shaking my head, I leaned in, kissing her neck and loving the little squeal that escaped her lips. "Tired of hearing that sexy sound? No way."

Smoothing my hands down her arms, I pulled them up over her head, pinning them to the floor as I rose above her. Her eyes were on my torso, and she licked her lips. "Your body looks like it's been sculpted by one of the masters."

I looked at her firm, plump tits. "Looks like God gave you two luscious scoops, baby."

Her laughter peeled through the air, and I rolled over, pulling her with me so she could take the top spot. With her hands checking out every inch of my chest, she rocked her body over mine. "I needed this. You have no idea how badly I've needed this."

"I have some idea." Running my hands up and down her arms, I could see total relaxation in her face for the first time.

She blushed a little then smacked my chest lightly. "I mean that I had a trying day at the hospital. There was this baby born last week. She was born with an addiction to meth. The state took away the mother's rights after the test came back positive. We've been taking complete care of this little girl since she was only a few hours old."

"That sounds so sad, baby." My heart ached for the poor kid. "How could a woman do that to her unborn child?" I couldn't wrap my head around that.

"It happens more than it should, that's for sure." One tear rolled down her cheek, and I wiped it away. She took my hand and kissed the palm. "That baby was the first and only baby that actually liked me. She liked me over everyone else too. And, to be honest, I gave a lot of thought into seeing if I could adopt her."

"Wouldn't caring for a child with such problems be incredibly difficult?" I had no real idea what happened to a baby born with an addiction of any kind. But I knew people who'd gone through hell with addictions.

"Yes, it would. There could be issues for the rest of her life. But, for a while, I thought about making her mine." She wiped another tear away. "But when I went to go hold her and feed her this morning, another woman was already there. She'd been sent by the Department of Human Services."

"Did she take the baby?" I knew she had. I could see the sorrow on her face.

Nodding, she wiped away more tears. "I'm happy for the baby. I really am. This woman and her husband have taken in two other babies who were born with the same addiction. She's got almost ten years of experience with them. She is what's best for that poor baby girl, and I know that. But knowing that doesn't make it hurt any less."

Pulling her to me, I hugged her, kissing the side of her

head. "Honey, I'm so sorry. I'm sure it does hurt. But you know that you don't have time to be what that baby needs. You have the heart — you most definitely have the heart — but you've got a great goal to accomplish. Once you become a doctor, you can help thousands, maybe even millions of people. People with all sorts of problems."

"I know," she said with a whimpering voice. "But she liked me. She. Liked. Me. None of the babies I've tried to comfort have."

"Maybe they will start liking you now. Maybe now there's something different about you. And maybe it's because we met that you have a calmness about you that you might not have had before." Wrinkling my nose, I realized I was sort of taking credit for something she'd done. "But that's all you, baby. For sure, it's all you."

"No, it's not all me. I think you might be right. I've been closed off for such a long time. Until you came along and started stalking me, I didn't even have anyone to think about."

"Stalking you?" I did not like how she'd put it.

Her brows rose as she wore a questioning expression, pushing herself up to a sitting position. "What would you call it?"

Lifting her to get her moving again, I thought about what one would call what I'd done. "Is it stalking if you think you might like someone and the only place you're sure to see them again is at the place you met?"

"I think that's the exact definition of stalking, Stone." She smiled, arching her back while running her hands through her hair. "But I'm glad you did it."

"Well, we are not going to call it stalking. We can call it being persistent. I like the sound of that." I liked that much better, actually. "So, when anyone asks you how we ended up together, you can say that I was persistent in my endeavors to make you mine."

"You have been that." Leaning in, she kissed my neck.

"Now it's my turn to be persistent. Only I'm going to persistently please you, my hunky lover."

I wanted to be so much more than just her lover. I wanted to be her one true love, the way she was mine. Not that I was about to tell her anything like that on our first date and first time having sex. That would just be stupid, although we'd spoken rather clearly about seeing love in each other's eyes. But still, it was too soon to start saying the words I love you. Yet, it would've been a nice thing to hear — for me at least.

Women had told me that they loved me, but most of them had been drunk, and many of them had just been trying to win my heart. Jessa hadn't even seemed to be trying to win my heart, but she sure as hell had.

Jessa hadn't been kidding about pleasing me, and she got to work sucking on my neck until I was so turned on that I rolled over, pinning her beneath me. "Get ready to come as close to Heaven as you'll ever get, baby."

Our mouths crashed together as I went for the finish line. When I made it, I felt a wave of something unusual bowl me over. For a minute, I couldn't even see. But when the blackness faded, there was Jessa's pretty face, red with the heat our bodies had created. "Wow," she said as she smiled. "Just wow, Stone."

"Yeah?" I was glad she seemed to have gotten a lot out of it too. "I thought it was pretty wow myself. I'm glad the blackness went away. I thought I might've gone blind there for a minute."

"You really put your all into it." She pulled me down to her, kissing me softly before she asked, "What if you and I find that we want to do this more often?"

"I can assure you that I will want to do this as often as you'll let me."

*Every night sounds great to me.*

# CHAPTER 22
## JESSA

Three weeks had passed since our one night together. It wasn't that I didn't want to spend more nights with Stone. The timing just wasn't right for either of us. He was busy getting things in order to open the bistro in the hospital, and that meant there was a hell of a lot of hoops he had to figure out how to jump through. And I had my usual hellish schedule. Midterms had me spending every available moment I had studying so that I could pass them.

In a rare moment, I saw Stone coming into the cafeteria as I was just about to finish the Italian burrito he'd sent samples of that afternoon. I'd come to the cafeteria to get a bottle of water to drink while eating, but I could see from the furrowed brow he was wearing that he'd assumed I'd eaten something from there. "What are you doing in here, young lady?"

Holding up the empty paper wrapper the burrito had been in, I smiled. "Not what you think."

The wrinkles along his forehead disappeared as he realized that I wasn't cheating on his food. "Good."

I tossed the trash into the bin then found his arms wrapped around me, his lips on mine. His kiss took my breath away, and I melted in his arms. "I have missed you."

"Me too, baby." He couldn't seem to let me go. "We have to make time for each other. I know you've got to take those tests. But when will you be done with them?"

"My last test is on Friday. And as soon as I'm finished with that, I have to get back to work. The day manager is working for me. She'll stay until I can come in."

"Are you working here on Saturday morning?"

"I am." I knew this time problem was a huge one. "I told you this wasn't going to be easy."

"Nothing easy is ever worth much." He swayed with me in his arms without letting go. "Sunday?"

"Well, since I'll be making the schedule on Friday night, I'll be sure to give myself Sunday night off. And with all my tests behind me, the next classes won't be starting for another week."

Excitement peppered his deep voice. "You're going to be free for a week?"

"Not entirely, no. But I'll have more free time than I normally would. I'll have two free nights when I take them off from Hamburger Hut." I held my breath, waiting to see what he would say to that.

"You're spending both those nights with me. As soon as you know what nights you're off, you let me know so I make sure to free myself up too. When you get off work here, you can go straight over to my place. I'll text you the codes to the gate and the front door."

"Wow, that's like giving me a key to your place. You sure you're ready to give up that much of yourself?" We hadn't spoken about being exclusive. I mean, he knew he was my exclusive since I could barely find time for him, much less for anyone else. "What if I show up one night, late and unannounced just so I can cuddle with you for a few hours, only to find another woman in your bed?"

Shaking his head, he said, "That won't happen."

"You sure?" I knew I wasn't giving him the amount of sex

he was used to. "A man has needs, but I'm not doing much to satisfy them."

"Don't worry about that." He kissed me softly. "I'm more than satisfied."

I wasn't going to lie. I wanted more of what he gave out so well. "I've gotta get back to work. Otherwise, I'd love to just stand here, letting you hold me in your strong arms." I put my hands on his muscular biceps, recalling how they flexed as he moved over me. Warmth spread through me, pulses in my lower regions signaling that arousal had already begun. And I didn't have time for that.

Leaning in, his breath flowed warmly over my ear, "How about a quicky in an empty patient room?"

"If I could, I would. Somehow, I don't think either of us would stop at a quicky."

"Yeah, you're right about that. I can hold out for those two nights you're spending with me." He grinned as his eyes lit up. "In my head, I'm already planning out the dinners for both nights."

"Nothing fancy," I said as I laughed, knowing full well the man knew no other way of making a meal — at least when he was making one for me.

"Never." With a sigh, he kissed my cheek then let me out of his arms. "Get back to work before I toss you over my shoulders and steal you away from this place, kicking and screaming."

"As if you would do such a thing." I reluctantly moved a few steps back, making space between us where before there'd been none. "I'll text you later."

"Looking forward to it." He stood there as I walked away.

I was halfway to the operating room, as one of the doctors was about to do an appendectomy, when I realized that I hadn't asked Stone why he was at the hospital. I knew he had his sister-in-law and niece bringing the food samples in. Other than that, he didn't have any business at the hospital.

One of the other interns, Miss Callahan, came up beside me. "You don't happen to have anything for cramps, do you?"

"Like Midol?"

"Yeah. Anything will do. I've got terrible cramps. My time of the month came early, or I would've had some on me."

I'd kept a small packet of two pills in my pocket as my time of the month was supposed to have come a few days ago. "You can have these. I don't feel any signs of mine showing up today." I found it funny how most of the women who worked closely together had their times of the month on a very similar schedule.

"Great. Everyone I've asked has taken theirs already. We're all on the same pattern here, it seems. I'm lucky yours is running late." She took the pills out of the packet and swallowed them, chasing them down with a drink from the bottle of water she carried. "I'll bring some tomorrow so you can keep your stash on you. When the time hits, it's awful."

"Maybe you're early and I'm late because of that new nurse who started working here last month. We're probably all going through some syncing process. How I hate mother nature sometimes."

"Me too." We headed into the scrub room, finding that quite a few others had gotten there before us.

I counted the others and found ten were already scrubbed in. "Crap. We're too late."

She didn't look upset at all. "Good. I won't be stuck in there for who knows how long. Guess I'll go check out the emergency department." Miss Callahan left, and I walked out right behind her.

"I'll go see the babies, I guess." I hadn't gone to pediatrics since the baby girl was taken away. I hadn't wanted to feel the same pain I'd felt when that woman left with her. But I knew that I'd eventually end up going to that room where I'd held her day after day, rocking or walking with her, holding her,

140

trying to make her feel like things were going to be okay. Even trying to share my love with her.

I wasn't sure if it was Stone or that poor baby girl who'd taught my heart how to show love. It didn't matter. The only thing that mattered was that I'd learned how to open my heart up and that Stone had come into it willingly.

Our mutual patience with each other was something that amazed me. I hadn't thought anyone could be that patient. As I walked toward the elevator to go up to the third floor, I heard Stone's voice, "So, I'll see you tomorrow?"

"Yeah, tomorrow," a woman said.

I stopped and peeked around the corner, not wanting him to see me as I listened in on their conversation. *Who is she?*

The woman faced me as Stone's back was turned to me. She looked to be in her late twenties and had a wonderful tan, flowing blonde hair, and green eyes. Slim and trim, I had to admit that she was beautiful. I also had to admit that sparks of jealousy were zapping me.

"I can't wait!" Stone said.

"Me too!" she said with such excitement.

Suddenly, she threw her arms around him, and they were standing there in the lobby, hugging each other.

*What the actual fuck?*

Leaning back against the wall, my heart pounded as I barely took a breath. I wasn't sure what it was that I'd just seen. *My Stone, wrapped in another woman's arms?*

Out of the corner of my eye, I saw Stone walking toward the exit door. He had his fist up, pumping it into the air as if he'd just made some tremendous accomplishment.

*What if he'd been secretly trying to get that woman to go out with him, and he's finally succeeded? What if he got what he wanted from me, and now he's going to see if he can conquer that other woman?*

My stomach turned on itself, and I ran to the nearest bathroom, promptly throwing up everything I'd just eaten. Gripping my stomach, I wondered if I was overreacting. The way Stone looked at me told me that he genuinely cared about me.

We'd even spoken some about love — seeing love in each other's eyes. If that was real, then why would he be seeking out another woman?

*Once a playboy — always a playboy.*

But he wanted to spend my nights off together — in *his* bed. What man would want that if they were going to be sleeping with another woman?

*A bad boy. I have fallen for a bad boy.*

He might've said he would text me the codes to the gate and the house, but that didn't mean he wouldn't be changing the codes after our two nights together. He'd obviously just gained a date with that woman, so he wouldn't be inviting her to his place so soon. Or so I hoped.

*What am I thinking? I can't continue seeing him if he's actively seeking out other women! And that one obviously works in the same hospital I work in. What's he thinking?*

Obviously, his subconscious wanted me to catch him in the act. That way, he wouldn't have to end things with me because I would definitely be the one ending them.

Looking at myself in the mirror, I saw fear. And I hated to see or feel fear. My period was late, and my man was seeing another woman.

I may well be completely fucked. But I had to make sure of that first. So I left the bathroom and walked across the street to the pharmacy to pick up the one thing I'd never thought I'd be purchasing.

I then went to the bathroom in the back of the pharmacy and did the test right then and there. The sooner I knew, the sooner I could start dealing with things.

There was no way I was going to let Stone Nash make me look like a fool in front of the entire hospital staff. Everyone had seen us together. Even without me saying much to anyone about our relationship, they all could see that we clearly had one.

*No matter what, I've got to break things off with him.*

The timer on my phone dinged, and I looked over at the little stick that lay on top of the toilet paper dispenser. "Fuck my life.

## CHAPTER 23
## STONE

On cloud nine, I felt like I floated through the rest of the day. There had been so much to do that I'd done nothing but run from place to place to get the proper legal documents ready to go for the following day.

I'd texted Jessa a couple of times, wanting to share with her my great news, but she hadn't gotten back to me. My plan was to go home, shower, change, and then go see her at Hamburger Hut to tell her the news in person.

Just as I walked through my door, my cell rang, and I saw it was Baldwyn. "Hey, big bro. What's up?"

"I've got our cousins here at my place. Come on over and make your case for the grant you're wanting. Plus, they've brought barbeque, and we're going to have a nice family meal all together."

"Great!" Things were falling into place at a speed that I couldn't have imagined. "I'll shower and change, then be right over."

"Prepare to stay the night because, you know, there's gonna be lots of drinking. Cash brought samples of the liquors he's been making. See you soon."

"Oh, hell yeah!" The night had just gotten even better.

Sure, I wouldn't be able to talk to Jessa until the next day, but that was okay. I could go see her at the hospital during one of her breaks and tell her everything then. I'd be up there anyway, signing papers.

An hour later, I walked into Baldwyn's home with a big smile on my face. "Hello, family!"

The living room was huge, but there were so many people in it that it felt on the smaller side. Everyone had brought their families along.

Making my way around the room, I greeted everyone personally before we were all called to the dining room to enjoy the meal our cousins had flown in.

Baldwyn sat at the head of the table with his wife, Sloan, sitting on his right. He took her hand in his. "Since all of us being together is such a rare occasion, I think that saying grace over the dinner would be nice. Can we all join hands?"

I sat at the other end of the table and took my niece Madison's hand as she sat on my right. On my left was sitting my sister-in-law Orla, who held my other hand. "I can't believe y'all came all the way from Ireland to be here, Orla. But I'm glad you did."

"Me too, Stone. This is great. I love big family gatherings." Her smile was radiant, and it wasn't lost on me why my brother Warner had followed her all the way to Ireland to make her permanently his.

"God, we'd like to thank you for this bounty," Baldwyn began. "Breaking bread with family is a gift that we are all thankful for. Our cousins have delivered the finest meats in Texas, the finest spirits in Texas, and the finest company in Texas, too. For that, we are grateful. Lord, we ask that you bless this food that will serve to nourish our bodies and our souls. Amen."

"Amen," I said, ready to dig into the food. "This smells so good."

Tyrell said, "Stone, why don't you tell us all about this

restaurant you're gonna open and what you want us to help with."

"Right now?" We usually didn't talk business unless we were all alone.

"Yeah, right now. From what I've heard, you've got some pretty amazing ideas, and we'd all like to hear about them," he said.

"Wow. Well, okay." I wasn't used to being the one with the amazing ideas, but I was the one in the spotlight for once. "So, I'm seeing this woman — she's an intern at one of the local hospitals. She's going to be a doctor."

"A doctor?" Orla asked as she nodded while picking up a rib. "Nice, Stone."

"I know, right?" I couldn't wipe the grin off my face. "So, this woman, her name's Jessa. She also works as a night manager at a fast food place. That's where we met."

Cohen chuckled as he reached for the barbeque sauce. "For once, Stone's late-night partying paid off."

"Kids, bro!" I didn't want the little kids in our family to think I was some sort of party animal. "But yeah, my not-so-good ways finally paid off for me. And, for the record, I haven't partied since I met her. She's a good influence on me, apparently."

"I agree," Warner said before he bit into a steak burger. "Yum!"

"This food is really great, you guys. Whisper Ranch is raising some prime beef," Ember said as she cut into a grilled steak.

"We do try," Jasper said with pride. "So, tell us the idea behind your restaurant, Stone."

"So, the idea behind this bistro — I'm not calling it a restaurant because it's not going to be that big — is that I'll only be serving healthy foods, but not the same old boring things that everyone is tired of. I've done tons of research on nutrition and have come up with some awesome items. I can fill egg roll wrappers with all sorts of things and fry them in coconut oil, giving them the feel of something that's not good for you, but *is* good for you in reality. Plus, it doesn't leave you feeling bloated or heavy, but at the same time, it doesn't leave you feeling hungry like you haven't eaten anything substantial enough to fill you up either."

"How many items are on your menu?" Cash asked.

"Okay, so the things you can get there are pretty much limitless. Think of a sandwich shop, like Subway. They have all these ingredients that the customer decides on. That's one part of how my thing's gonna be. You can choose between an egg roll and a burrito, and then you pick what you'd like inside of it. We move along the assembly line, putting in the things you want, and then we roll them up and drop them into the fryer for five minutes. While they're frying, the customer will pick from a variety of dipping sauces. On the menu, there will be my specialties for those people who can't make up their mind."

Sloan asked, "How come you aren't opening this at the resort first? Why the hospital?"

"The interns, nurses, and doctors who work there don't have access to the best foods. The cafeteria doesn't exactly cater to healthy diets. And I've visited all cafeterias at all the local hospitals here in Austin and found the only healthy choices are the same old things — salads, raw veggies, cheese cubes or sticks, those sorts of things. People are done with that tasteless stuff. So, they will go for the tastier things that are available to them. Unfortunately, the tastier the foods in the cafeterias are, the worse they are for you."

"So, you can only get egg rolls or burritos?" my sister-in-law Alexis, asked.

"No. I'll have other items that will be prepared fresh daily and will already be packaged, ready to eat. Daily sandwich specials will be offered too, using only sourdough bread. Again, they'll be ready-made, but fresh veggies can be added to them at no extra cost. Plus, they'll come with homemade sweet potato chips." I liked the nods I was getting from everyone. "There'll be breakfast foods in the morning, and then we'll switch to the other foods at ten. We'll be open from six in the morning until seven in the evening. Most hospitals end their visiting hours at nine, and I'd like to be all cleaned up and closed up by that time."

"Sounds like you've been working hard this last month or so," Tyrell said. "Glad to see that spark of passion in your eyes, Stone. Cohen told us that he's going to file for some grants for you once you're established. He said you'd like to talk to us about funding a grant until those kick in. So, what do you need money for?"

"Feeding the interns and the residents — those are doctors on the last legs of their journey to becoming independent doctors. The interns and residents work twelve-hour shifts. Sometimes it can even go longer. But they don't get paid by the hour. The interns make around thirty-thousand dollars a year. And the residents make around fifty thousand. This isn't the kind of money someone who works that many hours in any field would take home. It leaves some of them broke. And being broke means they buy cheap food. And cheap food isn't always the most nutritious."

Jasper asked, "So the grants are to cover the cost of the food you're going to serve?"

"No." I knew I wasn't great at explaining things. "The grants are to cover the costs of the free meals we'll give the interns and residents. Everyone else will pay full price. But I'm doing all I can to keep those costs as low as I can while still making a tidy profit."

Jasper was quick to offer, "You can have our fresh, organically grown veggies at cost."

"Wow!" That was some gift. "You sure about that, Jasper?"

"One hundred percent sure. All I ask is that you put up some signage that has our logo and web address on it so people can look us up online to buy our products. A hell of a lot of people can go through hospitals. The way you're talking, I'm guessing you plan on putting these little bistros in as many hospitals as you can."

"I sure am."

Tyrell held up one finger. "You got all the meats you want at cost too, cousin. Do the same thing for the meat that you do for the veggies, and we've got a deal."

"Holy shit!" I knew my cousins were generous, but I had no idea how generous they truly were. "Thank you, guys. This is such a blessing."

Cash nodded. "We've all been blessed, Stone. This whole thing came out of nowhere for us. And what you want to do is good. It's good for people, and it helps our medical staff too. Giving people who are giving up so much just to learn how to care for the sick and the injured is just the right thing to do. I'm behind you, man. Now, all we got to give is liquor. But I bet you can't sell it up there."

"Probably not. But I can put up signage for that too." I, too, could finally give something back, and that made me happier than I'd ever been.

I had to tell Jessa all this fantastic news. So, as soon as dinner was over and I'd gotten everyone to agree on the grant, I found a quiet spot to make a call to her.

The call went straight to voicemail, giving me the impression that she'd turned her phone off for some damn reason. But she was working at Hamburger Hut, so I began looking up that number. A television was on in the corner of the room. Some of the kids must've been watching it before they were called to dinner. So I went over to get the remote to turn it off.

The sound was down, but what I saw on the screen immediately grabbed my attention. Raymond Joseph Moxon was written underneath the picture of a nicely dressed, older man. I turned up the sound to hear the reporter say, "It's a sad day in North Carolina, where textile heir and multi-billionaire

Raymond Joseph Moxon has passed away from a sudden heart attack. His entire estate will be passed down to his only heirs, his daughters, Carolina Lily Moxon of Durham, North Carolina, where the family estate is located, and Carolina Jessamine Moxon, currently living in Austin, Texas, where she attends Dell Medical School."

I went to my knees as I suddenly felt as if all the air had left my lungs. "She's rich!"

A knock came to the door of my office and Tammy opened it. "Hey, you've got a call. Some woman is crying her ass off. She says she's been trying to call your cell, but it seems to be off."

"Who'd be calling me at ten at night?" I picked up the phone on the desk then pressed the flashing number one button. "Jessa Moxon here."

"Jessa," came my sister's tear-filled voice. "Thank God I got you. I told the media I'd already contacted you. It was a lie, I know. But I honestly thought I would get you before the ten o'clock news would come on. It was headline news, so they already put it out there. Did you see it?"

"See what?" By the sound of her voice, I knew it couldn't be good. My stomach tensed, and I instinctively put my hand over it, already feeling protective of the baby. At three weeks, it wasn't even considered a fetus yet — it was still an embryo. And it was the size of a tiny vanilla bean. But in my mind, I'd already been calling it a baby.

"Our father," she said, then gasped. "I still can't believe it."

"Believe what?" I hated how dramatic Lily could be. "Come on, Lily, just tell me what's happened."

"He's dead!" She wailed so loudly that I had to pull the phone away from my ear.

*No. I couldn't have heard her right.* "Lily, calm down and say that again."

"He's dead, Jessa. A heart attack. The jet's coming for you as we speak. You have to get to the airport right now. I need you, sister. I can't do this alone. You have to come right now."

"Dad's dead?" The shock had me feeling numb all over. "No. This can't be. He's healthy." My mind raced back to the last time I'd seen him. He'd gained weight. "Why couldn't you make sure he was eating right, Lily?"

"You can't blame me, Jessa Moxon! You're his daughter too. You should've made more time for him — for us. Come home, Jessa. Please, don't make me beg you."

"Of course, I'm coming home." I couldn't believe she thought I wouldn't go back for my own father's funeral. "I'll go to the airport now. See you soon."

Grabbing my things, I rushed out of the office. "Tammy, I need you to call one of the other managers. My father's died. I've gotta go to North Carolina. I don't know when I'll be back." I didn't know *if* I would be back. My father had many responsibilities, and now those would all be falling on Lily and me. And I knew Lily wasn't up to any of what was about to hit us.

With a full heart, I drove like a demon to the airport, not bothering to stop by my apartment to get anything. I had plenty at our family home anyway. I had to get home. I had to see my father one last time before they put him in the ground.

*Why didn't I call him more often?*

Guilt tugged at my heart as I parked my car in the long-term parking lot then ran as fast as I could, somehow sensing that the jet was already waiting for me.

I'd been right about the jet and saw the pilot sitting in a chair at the gate. "Miss Jessa, I've been calling your cell to let you know that I was here. I'm so sorry about your daddy." He opened his arms to give me a hug. But I knew that would only serve to put me into hysterical tears.

"Sorry, Mr. Peterson. No hugs. I'm not prepared for them yet." I moved past him to get onto the family plane. A plane I'd often ridden in with my father as he'd come along to pick me up most of the time.

"I understand, honey." He followed me quietly as I ran up the stairs, stopping as I got just inside the aircraft.

Daddy's seat sat empty, and I felt a knot form in my throat. I would never again see him sitting there, waiting for me to board and go back home with him. "I'm sorry." I wiped my eyes as I went to take a seat beside his.

The pilot had been with us since before I was even born. He knew our family well. "He loved you, you know. And he was damn proud of you too, Miss Jessa. He told everyone how you were going to come back home, a real doctor."

One tear fell down my face, and then more and more gushed until I could no longer hold back what had been damming up inside of me. "I loved him too. I'm sorry." I tried to suck it up, remain the ever-strong person I'd always been. "I'm so sorry."

He leaned over, put something in my hand, then hugged me. "Here's some tissues. I'm gonna leave you alone and get you back to your home, Miss Jessa. You go on and cry all you want. It's natural to cry at a time like this."

I lost track of time as sorrow took over. I found my hand on my stomach more often than not. "I'm sorry for everything," I told my little vanilla bean. "I'm sorry I've brought you into a world that you might not be ready for. I'm sorry I didn't think about what would happen if I brought a kid into all this. I'm sorry I did this to you. But I swear to you that I'll do my best to do what's right for you. I'll just have to put myself on the backburner for now. I can do that."

Being under the stress of losing my father couldn't be good for the baby. But there wasn't a damn thing I could do about it.

I looked up, wishing I could see straight through that plane and the night sky, right up to Heaven. Dad was once again with his wife, our mother. It had been such a long time that he'd lived without her.

I knew they were happy, even if they'd left behind two daughters who loved them. Lily and I had had Dad to ourselves for long enough. It was time our mother had him.

It wasn't just that I'd lost my father. It was so much more than that. There would be so much to do, and things wouldn't stop after he was buried and the funeral was over either. I'd lost my life in a very real way. Unless my sister would step up to take things over.

That was going to be a longshot. Lily was spoiled and hadn't wanted to learn a damn thing. But she did have a college education. She had a bachelor's degree in Business. Daddy had made sure she'd completed college. He wasn't about to have either of his kids go without proper education. It wasn't as if my older sister was dumb. She was able to learn. She just didn't want to do anything other than shop and socialize. And our father never saw fit to try to push either of us to do anything more than graduate from college.

In a way, he'd left my sister in such a state that it would leave me to carry the burden of keeping the money we'd inherited moving and growing. I couldn't keep up with school and the internship if I were to oversee all he'd overseen. My life as I knew it — my dream — was over.

For now, my tears had dried, leaving my eyes swollen and my heart waterlogged. There would be so much to do in the coming days, that I knew I'd have this chance to talk to Stone, and that would be about it.

I wasn't going to bring up what I'd seen. It didn't even matter now, anyway. He had a right to be with anyone he wanted. I wouldn't be there anymore.

I couldn't expect him to uproot and follow me to North Carolina. He'd just found his passion, and his life was in

Austin. He'd been working so hard, and he'd come so far in a short amount of time, too.

He would need to move on, and so would I. And that made my shattered heart ache even more.

It was late, but I made the call anyway. I had to turn my cell phone back on, angry at myself for turning it off in the first place. I'd handled things in an immature way. That wasn't like me.

It may have been jealousy or the pregnancy hormones that had me acting so childishly. Whatever it was, it no longer mattered.

"Jessa," he answered my call. "Baby, where are you? I went to your work, and Tammy said you'd left. I know about your father. I'm so sorry, baby."

"Thank you." It felt good just to hear his voice. "I'm on my way home now." The fact that he knew about my father let me know that he likely now knew that I was wealthy and had come from money. "Do you hate me for calling you out when I found out that you had money?"

"I could never hate you, Jessa. I don't understand why you hid this from me. And I really can't understand why you've been working at that crappy job to pay for college, either," he sighed. "But you don't have to answer anything right now. This is about you and your loss. I want to be with you. I know you need me to be with you."

I did need him. But I didn't want to need him. "I've got to do this on my own. And there's more to it than that, Stone. Things in my life are going to change drastically now. My sister won't be able to run my father's business. It's going to be up to me to do it. And I'm pretty sure it might always be that way. Leaving North Carolina isn't going to be in the cards for me anytime in the foreseeable future."

"I still want to be there for you, baby. We'll deal with things as they come." He cleared his throat, giving me the impression that he was getting choked up. "Jessa, I don't want to lose you."

Despite everything, I couldn't stay quiet about what I'd seen him do earlier that day. "Stone, I saw you with that woman today."

"Ah, I get it now. You turned your phone off because you were upset with me. I should've known. I thought you would know who she was. But I guess you didn't."

"Who is she? And why would that matter anyway? You were hugging another woman, and both of you were over the moon about your date tomorrow." I bit my lower lip, trying not to resume crying again.

"Our date tomorrow is about signing the papers for the bistro inside the hospital. She's the foodservice administrator. I've been working with her to get the space. And the hug she gave me came out of nowhere. I chalked it up to her just being excited for me. I'm sorry you took it the wrong way, baby. That makes me feel terrible."

It made me feel pretty terrible too. "Shit. I'm sorry I jumped to conclusions. I should've been an adult about it, instead of hiding and eavesdropping. I should've joined you and talked to you."

"None of that matters now. Don't even think about it."

"I won't. But it's nice to know that you weren't screwing around on me."

"Not in a million years, Jessa. No way. You've got me in the palm of your hands."

"Stone, I don't want you to take this the wrong way, but I've got to put some things on the backburner for a while. For how long, I don't even know. You and I are included in that. I have other things to think about for now. Please, tell me that you understand. Things might never be the same again."

*But I wish they could be.*

# CHAPTER 25
## STONE

Grief can make people act like someone they're not. That was the case with Jessa. All the drive she seemed to have had disappeared with the death of her father. I knew a thing or two about losing one's parents. Of course, I was just a little kid when I'd lost mine, but I was sure Jessa felt a lot like I did back then. I'd felt alone in the world, at first. I did have my brothers, and Jessa had an older sister. Just knowing that there's someone here on Earth who shares your blood makes a hell of a lot of difference. But it takes time to come to that conclusion.

I'd barely slept at all that night, and as soon as the sun rose, I got out of bed and put my clothes on, joining my oldest brother, Baldwyn, downstairs for a coffee in the breakfast room. "Hey, Baldwyn. Thanks for throwing that great party last night. Sorry I disappeared on y'all. I got a call from Jessa last night and really didn't feel much like talking after that."

"You said her father passed away. I'm sure she was upset about that. Who wouldn't be?" He blew across the surface of the coffee, making steam twirl above the surface like a mini-tornado.

That's how I felt inside — like a tornado was running amuck through my body and mind, pretty much tearing up everything within its reach. "I told her I would go to her, but she doesn't want me to. She said I need to stay here and deal with everything I've got going on right now. But the thing is, my heart is already with her, and my mind can't even think straight. She's going to have loads to deal with. I know she needs me right now."

"You have to let her do things the way she wants to, Stone. You said that she works at some fast food place as a night manager to help pay her way through medical school. Someone who's gone that far to avoid telling everyone that she's got tons of money must have a reason. If she doesn't want you to be there with her, I'm sure she has her reasons."

"I'm sure she has her reasons too. But I don't care about any of them. I know she needs me right now, and she's just being stubborn about it. She's got this thing about acting like she's the strongest person in the world. Her self-discipline is off the charts. And she said she needs to move us to the backburner for now, and who knows how long that will last. I can't take that."

Baldwyn shook his head as his expression turned grim. "Look, you've gotta accept what she's said. And you do have a hell of a lot that you need to do. Today you've got to meet with the hospital board to finalize the details of your lease. And you need to be on top of your game, or they could refuse you."

I couldn't let everything go. My brother was right. "How do I shove this horrible feeling to the side so I can deal with the things I have to today?"

"It's important to you, isn't it?"

"Extremely." But so was Jessa. "What about Jessa, though?"

"She's with family and friends. She's as fine as she can be right now. You know how things like that work. It takes time to get back to who you were before a parent dies. Even if you're right there by her side every minute of the day and night, it won't take her pain away. It'll make you feel better, sure, but you know that you'll be there, thinking about what you're giving up back here."

"I could postpone things." That was a viable option.

His chest rose and fell with a heavy sigh. "Look, I want you to succeed. It doesn't matter when you succeed, but I know you can do it, and I want you to make that a priority. Now, I know that when a woman gets under your skin, it's next to impossible to shut that feeling off. I get it. But this situation is different. Jessa has lost her father, which means she won't be the same person for the next little while. That's just how grief works. And you shouldn't put things off with your own life to wait around for when or if she even goes back to being the girl you knew and fell for."

"Baldwyn, I love her," I admitted. "I've never met anyone like her. I've never felt so completely connected to anyone the way I feel with her. And her not wanting me with her just so I don't miss out on an opportunity to start a business that, let's face it, I can start at any time, shows me how truly selfless she is. She's the one, brother. She. Is. The. One. And I know that without a shadow of a doubt."

"You sound pretty sure about that. And I'm not saying that you're wrong. But have you thought about the fact that she might have to stay with her sister for a while? Where did you say she's from?"

"North Carolina. I did my research and found out that the Moxon Estate is in Durham. The date of the funeral hasn't been set yet." My brother was right, but I had yet to wrap my head around it. "She did say that she'll have to stay there, and she had no idea how long that would be. She also said that things might never be the same."

"Well, then you have your answer. You can't expect her to be able to return to life as you two have known it. You can become innovative about this, or you can try to understand that this is the end for you two, at least for the next year or so."

He was insane if he thought I could merely accept that.

"Baldwyn, I won't let that happen. I will not lose her to some family obligations. There are things I can do. I can keep on going forward with the bistro. And I can jet over to see her once a week too. It's not like we don't have our own jet."

Nodding, he agreed, "You could do that."

"Hell, we've been seeing each other for around six weeks now, and in all that time, we've only had one real date, and she's only stayed over one night." I thought that showed we had a special relationship that didn't rely on sex to keep us together.

"Hold on." He looked at me with disbelief in his eyes. "Are you telling me that in the last six weeks, you've only had sex once?"

"I said one night. We had sex multiple times that night. And we were supposed to spend two nights out of this coming week together too. I was looking forward to that." And now there would be none for a good while. But I was fine with that. I understood that she wouldn't be into that with her father having just passed away so unexpectedly.

"Huh. You really are committed to this girl. I have to admit that." Tapping his fingers on the table, he seemed to be thinking.

"Baldwyn, I can go to that meeting today, and I can be on my A-game. But after that's over, I can go to North Carolina later today or even tomorrow. Things might get started a bit later than planned, but they *will* get started. I've got to go to her."

With one brow cocked, he asked, "And if she refuses to invite you?"

"I must hope she'll eventually want me with her and stop being such a selfless person, at least for a while, so I can be there for her to lean on."

"It might be a good idea for you to go, actually. I'm sure her father had trusted advisors or at least one person who assisted him with whatever his endeavors were. She might not be thinking clearly enough to ask them for help. You might be able to see things she can't right now. But you can't go without her having invited you. That would be offensive, I would think."

Nodding, I guessed he was right. "I've gotta get home and get ready for that meeting. I'll let you know how it goes. And thanks for the advice."

"No problem. I'm a phone call away if you need anything."

"Thanks."

I left his place to get to mine and saw that it was already nine in the morning. I knew it was an hour later in North Carolina, so I called Jessa's cell to see if she would answer. "Come on, baby, talk to me."

"Stone?" she asked with a teary voice.

"It's me, baby."

"Oh, Stone," she sobbed.

"Baby, it's going to be okay. I'm coming to you very soon," I tried to console her.

"No!" she shouted. "You can't do that. You've got the bistro to open. There's so much for me to do now anyway. And my sister," she wailed, "my sister seems incapable of handling the smallest things. She wouldn't go to the funeral home with me to pick out his coffin and make the funeral arrangements. I had to go alone. And they had his body in the freezer, Stone. The God-forsaken freezer. They said they didn't know how long we'd want to wait before the funeral. They said a lot of times people of his importance allow a week's time for people to fly in to be at the funeral."

"Honey, your father doesn't care about that or feel any pain. He's not in that body anymore, and you know that." My heart ached for her. All I wanted to do was be there to hold her. "Baby, let me come and help you with everything."

"You can't do that. I won't let you kill your dream because of my father's death. I would never forgive myself for letting my ordeal take away or adversely affect your dream. Stone, it's a great idea, and it's going to help many people. You standing by my side won't help anyone but me."

"I will help *you*. And *you're* all I care about right now. Let me decide what I'm willing to sacrifice for you, Jessa," I begged her.

"I won't let you sacrifice a thing for me, Stone Nash. I won't do it!"

"Listen to me. There's more than one way for me to do this thing. I'm going to the meeting today, and I'm going to get the space leased. Once that's done, I can take a few days to come be with you. Then I'll come back and get going on things. We can still make this work, baby."

"Stone, I'm not myself right now."

"I know that. I understand that. I haven't told you this, but my parents died when I was a kid. I know what you're going through."

"God, Stone. Why haven't you told me that?" She sounded even more upset somehow.

"We've had little time to talk about things. And it's not something that I wanted to bring up." I knew there was a lot we needed to talk about. We barely knew a thing about each other. "But we have plenty of time to get to know all there is to know about each other."

"You know that time has always been against us, Stone. And I'm afraid that's never going to change. So, I've made an extremely hard decision."

"You should not be making any decisions right now, Jessa." I clenched my jaw, as I felt something big about to happen.

"Stone, my life isn't my own anymore. I'm not going to be able to finish my degree. I'm not going to achieve my dream of becoming a doctor. I've got to take over from where my father left off. I can't drag you away from your family and your dream. So, this is it, Stone. This is the last time we're going to talk to one another. I'm going to block your number as soon as I hang up."

"Jessa, don't!" I pulled to the side of the road, my heart about to pound out of my chest. "Don't do that. I have to be able to talk to you."

"It's for the best, Stone. There's no reason to drag this out and for you to end up in this pit with me. But I don't want you to think for one second that I don't love you because I love you more than I knew I was capable of loving anyone. And it's because of that love that I'm setting you free instead of trapping you here with me."

Tears filled my eyes, and I was certain she heard them in my voice as I begged her, "Jessa, please don't do this. I love you too. I need you, baby. Please, just stop thinking this way."

"I'm sorry. I can't drag you down with me. Goodbye."

"No!"

She ended the call, and I immediately called her back, only to find that she had indeed blocked my number.

*Holy, mother of God, I think I'm going to die!*

# CHAPTER 26
## JESSA

The phone call had taken a toll on me, and I couldn't pull myself together as I laid face-down in my bed, crying my heart out. My selfish side wanted to tell Stone to come to me and get here as fast as he could. I was in over my head — I knew that without a doubt. But the other part of me was bigger and wouldn't allow my weaker side to pull the man I loved away from his goals.

*If only I could just get Lily out of bed to help me, then this wouldn't be as hard as it is.*

Rolling over, I wiped my eyes with the heels of my hands then went across the hall to my sister's suite. Throwing open the door, I found her wilted in a chair, her blonde hair in a messy bun atop her head, staring blankly out of the window. The pale, yellow curtain blew with the gentle breeze. The sight mesmerized me. "It's a beautiful day."

"I wouldn't know."

"Lily, you're looking out of the window. Of course you know that it's a beautiful day outside. You and I should be out there, taking in the sunshine and visiting with the people who've come to pay their respects. The staff and Daddy's close friends have been taking care of what is ours to see to."

"I can't do it," she moaned as her eyes rolled to mine. "Jessa, I wasn't meant to go through something like this."

"You're younger than our father, so one day, you would have most certainly had to go through this." I hated how weak she was. "Lily, you are the oldest child. You should be the one trying to console me, not the other way around. There's tons of stuff to do, and I need your help."

"I've already told you that I can't do anything. Don't count on me, or you'll only be disappointed." Her lower lip began to tremble. "I still can't believe he did this to me. Leaving me here like this."

"He didn't do it on purpose." I took a seat on the small sofa in her bedroom.

"It doesn't matter," she said with a whimper. "I don't know how to do anything. How can I help with any of this?"

"You can learn," I pointed out. "You can try."

"I can't. I don't have the heart to try. I feel so alone, Jessa. You have no idea."

I had every idea. "You think I don't feel alone? Lily, you are of no comfort to me at all. In fact, you seem to be another burden that I have to bear, and I've already got plenty as it is. Can't you just suck it up and be a team player for once?"

"Like I even know how to do that." She put her hands over her face to cover it. "I can't even be seen right now. My eyes are red and puffy from all the crying. I feel bloated like I'm about to get a visit from Aunt Flo on top of everything else."

That did it for me. "Poor little Carolina Lily might get her period. What a shame. Well, then please allow me to do *everything*!" I hadn't told a soul what I'd found out, but I thought my sister should know. "Lily, I'm pregnant."

Her hands slowly fell from her face, revealing raised brows and large blue eyes. "You are not. You're just saying that to make me feel like I have to help you. But you don't understand that I have no clue how to go about doing anything Daddy did."

"I *am* pregnant. I only found out yesterday. I'm three weeks pregnant with my little vanilla bean. That's how big the embryo is right now." I ran my hand over my flat stomach. "And I know that you don't know how to do anything our father did. But you should know that I don't know how to do any of it either. I've been away at school, learning how to become a doctor, not take over a multi-billion-dollar estate."

She looked at my stomach. "Three weeks. How can you know that for sure?"

"I've only had sex once, and that was three weeks ago."

"Once?" She stared at my stomach. "With who?"

"With a very handsome man. A very wonderful man with a talent for cooking. He's a chef on the verge of becoming a great success. And that's why I won't be telling him about our baby. He shouldn't let me or the mess that's now going to come along with me trap him into a life that won't ever live up to his dream." My heart thudded like a brick in my chest. It wasn't happy with me or my decisions.

"His name, Jessamine," she said. "Tell me his name."

"It's not like you'll know him, Lily. But his name is Stone Nash. Along with being the best chef in the whole world, he and his four older brothers own a resort in Austin. They were even featured in a magazine. Believe it or not, I have fallen in love with a billionaire."

"Not you," she scoffed. "You hate men with money."

"I did hate men with money. But I love this one. And that's why I set him free this morning, right after I got back from the funeral home, which you should've come with me to, to make the arrangements. I have no idea how far people might be coming to attend his funeral. They have our father on ice to keep his body as fresh as they can, as they assumed we wanted to wait at least a week before burying him."

"Of course, that's what people of his social stature do. I hope you agreed with them on that." She dabbed the corners of her eyes.

"You are wrong. I told them to get him out of the freezer and begin the embalming process as soon as they possibly could. I won't let him stay like that. And I've set the date for three days from now."

She looked horrified as she sat upright instead of slumping. "Jessa, what have you done? No one will understand this rush. And I won't look even halfway decent in a mere three days. A week would've given my eyes some time to return to normal. You've already ruined this — and in such a short time!"

"See why you should've come with me?" I wasn't going to apologize for a damn thing. "And you won't have three days before going out in public either. The viewing will be in two days, and you *will* attend."

"Two days?" I'd seen my sister's mortified expression more than once in my life, since she was so quick to go to dramatics. "I can't possibly do that. I'll call the funeral home and make changes to the schedule."

"No, you won't." I wasn't going to have her do nothing, only then to go in and undo the things I'd done. "You were given plenty of time to get ready to come with me this morning. You made your choice, and now that's how things are. If you want to be a part of making these decisions, then I suggest you get showered and dressed and get your ass downstairs where I will be deciding on the rest of the arrangements with the help of our father's esteemed colleagues."

"You don't seem to be listening to me. I cannot face people yet. You may not have a reputation to uphold, but I still do. No one can see me looking like this."

"Everyone down there has the same red, swollen eyes, sister. You will be in good company, I assure you." She was such a diva. "Wear sunglasses if you want to. It's not like anyone will call you out on it."

"No." She slumped back in the chair. "I have no choice but

to let you take care of everything. At the end, when people ask about why everything is going to hell, I'll simply blame you."

"You are a shitty, shitty older sister. I want you to be completely aware of that fact." Fury had built up to the point of spewing out of my mouth. I was tired of trying to get her to do something she clearly wouldn't. "I've got the weight of the world on my shoulders, and you don't care. I've got a baby coming, and there will be no father for it. Neither will there be a man for me. But I'm going to go through with it anyway. And you — well, you can't even pull yourself together enough to go downstairs to let the people who have been in our lives since birth share their grief with us and offer their condolences. You say you're a high-standing member of this socialite society. Well, right now, you're the member of nothing — not even the human race, in my opinion."

"How dare you speak to me that way, Carolina Jessamine Moxon. You have no idea the weight that's on my shoulders. I carry the weight of ignorance. I carry the weight of knowing, without a single doubt, that I will be a burden to you now. And if you care to know this about your older sister, I've recently realized that I was a burden to my father too."

"*Our* father, and yes, you were." I saw no reason to try to make her think otherwise. "Time to grow the fuck up. He might not have taught you how to do a damn thing, but I will. Or I will simply stop trying to keep this estate afloat. It's as easy as that."

With her hand on her chest, she seemed genuinely stupefied. "You would let all our money dwindle away instead of tending to things as Daddy did?"

"If you don't come around and start trying to be a part of the team, then I will have no choice. I have a child to think about. I will not run my body into the ground to take care of your ass either. I will live to see my baby, and I will live to raise her or him. And I won't let anyone get in the way of achieving that goal — unlike my dream of becoming a doctor, which has been completely derailed." I could take no more. I ran back to my bedroom to let the tears that had been burning the backs of my eyes run free.

*Damn you, Daddy, for spoiling rotten your oldest daughter — rotten to her very core!*

# CHAPTER 27
## STONE

Three days had passed since Jessa broke up with me and blocked my number. I'd accomplished more in those three days than I knew I could. I'd signed the lease at the hospital and hired my sister-in-law Sloan, to hire and oversee a crew to put together the layout she'd come up with for the bistro. And now, I was on my way, in our company plane, to Durham, North Carolina.

Thanks to the internet, I'd found the address of the Moxon family estate. I knew there was no way of knowing how she'd take my arrival, but I was ready to take a gamble on Jessa being happy to see me. She'd told me that she loved me — that had to mean she still had deep feelings for me. They couldn't possibly have gone away that fast.

As soon as the plane landed, I rented a car and put the address into the GPS system. At the first traffic light that I got to, where I was supposed to take a left, I found a police officer on a motorcycle stopping traffic to let cars cross through the intersection. "Great, a funeral procession going down the same road I've gotta take."

After ten minutes, the line ended, and the cop got on his motorcycle and followed behind them. I made the turn and slowly proceeded down the road. The GPS showed that I would be taking a right in only a mile, so I tried my best to be patient, knowing the line of cars in the funeral procession wouldn't be going that way. That road was a private one that lead to the Moxon Estate.

But when I got closer to that turn, the cars continued going down the private road. It had to be Jessa's father's funeral. And the fact that they were going to the estate told me that he would be buried on their land. A shudder ran through me as I thought about how sad it would be for Jessa to see her father's tombstone every time she looked out of some window from the house.

Knowing that Jessa had attended the funeral without me made me feel like I'd waited too long to come to her. But there was nothing I could do about that now. I could only help her from here onwards.

I parked the car with everyone else's, as men in black suits pointed us to park. Getting out, I took a moment to look at the grand old mansion. It looked like a picture out of a magazine. White columns all along the front of the mansion held up a balcony that went from one side of the massive house to the other. Moss hung from giant oak trees, and the perfectly cut grass was the deepest shade of green that I'd ever seen grass be.

Although lovely, I could see why Jessa wouldn't have felt at home in a place like this. It looked more like a museum than a home where people raised their children.

Pulling my attention from the grandeur of the historical mansion, I followed the people as they went around the side of the house. And then I heard the sound of a woman crying. Looking around, I saw someone sitting on stone steps that led to a door. Her hands covered her face, but she had long blond hair that hung around her shoulders. A black dress went all the way to her feet, and pointy black shoes peeked out from beneath it.

I had no idea who she was, but her cries were so pitiful that I couldn't stop myself from going to her. I gently placed my hand on her shoulder. "It's going to be okay, you know."

Her hands moved slowly away from her face, and she looked up at me with red, swollen eyes. "How do you know that?"

"Because I've gone through what you are going through now. Only it was many years ago, when I was just a kid and lost both my parents. You *will* survive this. And you *will* be stronger for it."

Eyeing me warily, she asked, "And just who are you, wise man?"

"My name is Stone Nash, and I'm here to find Jessa Moxon."

Jumping up in a sudden flash, she wrapped her arms around me. "Thank God you came!" She let me go, her eyes as wide as saucers. "She needs you more than you will ever know. This is all too much for her — for us. She's in over her head. We both are. Only I *know* I am, but she keeps pretending she's not."

"That's my Jessa." I smiled, hoping like hell that Jessa would be happy to see me. "Since you're lumping yourself in with her, can I assume that you're her sister, Lily?"

"Oh, I forgot to introduce myself. How silly of me." She held out her hand as if she expected me to take it and kiss it, something that I guessed was some sort of North Carolina tradition. "I am Carolina Lily Moxon, Stone Nash. It's a pleasure to make your acquaintance."

I took her hand and placed a kiss on top of it. "I do believe I'm supposed to say that the pleasure is all mine. Right?"

"Yeah, you're right," she said as she laughed a little. "That's the first time I've laughed since..." She snapped her mouth shut.

"It's okay to laugh. Your father would be happy to hear his daughter's laughter. I'm sure he would. Parents don't like hearing their kids cry. They much prefer hearing their laughter. Or that's how it goes with my brothers and their kids, anyway. It's not like I have kids to know those kinds of things for myself."

For a moment, she just stared at me without saying a word. Then she looked around as if to make sure no one could hear what she was about to say. She took my hand and pulled me closer to her. "It's hard to know if my sister will tell you about this. She's told me she let you go so you wouldn't get pulled down into this with her. But you should know. You should definitely know."

"Know what?" I felt a bit confused. "That she loves me? Cause I know that, and she knows that I love her too. Jessa is too selfless. I'm here to try to show her that she can lean on people too. It won't make her weak."

"Not that." She looked around nervously. "God, she might kill me for telling you this. But in her present state of mind, I just know she won't do it. She's got to always be the strong one and won't let anyone help her. She keeps yelling at me to help, but I know she won't really let me do anything. It's not like I know more than she does about anything anyway. She is most definitely the smartest out of the two of us. But she needs your help, Stone. She truly does. Don't let her tell you otherwise. You'll have to be one hell of a man to get her to let you be there for her. But I think you can do it. Especially if you're sharing something that substantial."

Again, I felt confused. "If you're afraid of telling me something that your sister has asked you not to, and that might make her angry at you, then I don't want to get between the trust you two have with each other." The last thing I wanted was to start things off with Jessa by getting between her and her sister.

"She didn't tell *me* not to tell you. She just said that *she* wasn't going to tell you because it would make you feel obligated to stay in her life, a life that won't be very good, she thinks. Or something like that. I'm not sure what her exact words were. But the thing is, she's so worried about dragging you away from something. I think she said you're a chef and that you're going to do something with that. I'm not sure. I've been crying a lot, as you can imagine. Anyway."

"Anyway, really, Lily. I don't want you to tell me something that will start a conflict between you two. Right now, it's imperative to keep your bonds tighter than they've ever been before. She's all you have in the world now, and you're all she has."

I trusted Jessa would tell me anything that I really needed to know. Plus, I had the idea that, with her father gone, Lily was rather desperate for anyone to step in and take over. But I knew Jessa didn't want that. I'd be damn lucky if she would let me help at all. But I knew she wouldn't let me take over. Not that I would even want to. I'd made a promise to myself that I would fulfill my passion and keep moving forward with all the plans I'd made for the bistro, and the ones that would come after.

Nodding, she looked at how the people were beginning to thin out as everyone had gone around to the back of the house. "We should get going, or we'll miss the graveside service. You will accompany me."

She held her hand out, and I took it, tucking it into my elbow. "Of course." I figured I might as well learn how a gentleman in the south was supposed to act. "Y'all are very formal over here, aren't you?"

"You all, is how we say it here in North Carolina, Stone. Y'all sounds so common. And yes, we still have many formalities here." She smiled at me as we stepped around the side of the house. "I know my sister and I are complete opposites."

I saw a large structure in the middle of a garden in the backyard. "Is that a tomb?"

"It's called a mausoleum. Daddy's final resting place." She

dabbed the corners of her eyes. "It's the way he wanted it. See, our mother is in there. Daddy built this garden around the mausoleum he'd made for Momma and him. That's why it's so big. There's room for six more bodies in there. I've always thought I would be laid to rest within those marble walls. And you should know that Jessamine wants to be laid to rest there as well. She wants to take the place next to our mother, since she never got to be with her in her life. She wants to be with her on the other side."

"What do you mean?" I felt confused yet again.

"Our mother died giving birth to my baby sister."

"Oh, wow." My heart felt as if it had stopped. "That's terrible."

"Yes, it is." She dabbed her eyes again. "I'll take the place on our father's other side, since he and Mother are taking the two middle positions. And now I suppose the place on the other side of Jessamine will go to her child." She looked at me with wide eyes. "Oh, my. I guess the cat's out of the bag."

I still didn't understand what she was talking about. "What cat?"

"Oh, Stone, you are as clueless as you are handsome. My sister is carrying your baby. She found out the same day our father died. There wasn't any time to tell you about it."

I felt someone coming up on my other side as my mind spun like a top. "How come the last two times I've seen you, you've had some other woman wrapped around you, Stone Nash?"

*How come you haven't told me that I'm gonna be a father?*

His lips were slightly parted and his blue eyes darted back and forth as he looked at my stomach. "You're carrying my baby?"

I glared at Lily. "You told him?"

She nodded. "I did. But don't be mad. He needed to know. It wouldn't be right for him not to know. And I knew you wouldn't tell him."

Stone took me by the shoulders. "Hey, don't be mad at her. I'm kinda glad about this. It's only been a minute, and the idea of us having a baby has already grown on me."

He slipped his hands down my arms, taking one hand in his. I didn't know what the hell to say, so I said, "Oh. I guess that's good." I did feel a ton of relief with him knowing.

He kissed me on the forehead. "Everything is gonna be okay, baby."

Nodding, I still wasn't sure about that. Lily came to my other side and took my hand. "Come, let's get to the front where we belong."

I didn't let go of Stone's hand. "You're coming with me now that you're here."

"I'd like that." He held my hand as Lily led us through the crowd.

As soon as we got to the front, standing in front of the large mausoleum our father was about to be put in, my legs began to shake. Stone moved closer so I could lean against him.

The preacher led a prayer, one that I barely heard, as I waited for the moment to come when I would finally see my mother's casket for the very first time. Our father wouldn't ever let us open the doors to see it, saying he didn't want to disturb her eternal rest.

The pallbearers pulled the casket with my father's body from the back of the black suburban that had driven him to his final resting place. Two men from the funeral home unlocked the mausoleum's doors and opened them.

I couldn't pull my eyes off what was inside. The place was large enough to be able to walk around. There were six solid marble tables upon which the caskets rested. Only the middle one, the one right in front of us, was taken. A silver casket sat on top of that table, remnants of dried flowers sprinkled over the marble floor beside it. At the very end of the casket, I saw a simple gold band dangling from a gold chain that had been hung around one of the many handles that ran around the casket.

My throat ached with the lump that had lodged there. But I didn't want to cry. I wanted to take it all in and see it very clearly. Lily wept at my side, leaning against me as she kept a tissue on her eyes.

I looked up at Stone, who smiled at me. "That's my mom in there."

He nodded. "Lily filled me in."

I nodded too. "I've never seen this. It's the first time."

He let my hand go and wrapped his arm around my shoulder, pulling me in even closer as he kissed the top of my head. "Take it all in, honey. This memory will last you a lifetime."

The preacher said some more things that I couldn't hear over the thoughts floating inside my head. Then I watched as the six men carried my father's coffin into the chamber, placing him next to my mother. At the end of his casket, a simple gold band dangled from a gold chain just like my mother's. "Those are their wedding rings," I told Stone.

Lily made a loud sob. "They're together now, and no one will ever be able to separate them again."

It felt as if a knife had been plunged into my heart, as I knew that I'd been the one who separated them. "I'm so sorry."

Stone hugged me even tighter. "Don't blame yourself, baby."

There was no one else to blame. And that left me in tears. I heard Lily crying hard, then her hand left mine, and I looked to see our mother's sister, Aunt Lucy, pulling her into her arms, trying to comfort her.

I buried my face in Stone's chest, sobbing uncontrollably as they closed the doors, locking them up once more. "I can't take this."

Stone rocked with me. "This will all be over soon. You're going to be okay. Just try to breathe."

I didn't even feel myself moving, but when I finally pulled myself together enough to pull my head off Stone's chest, we were in my mother's old office. Dad hadn't changed a thing about it.

As I stepped away from him, Stone held out a small package of tissues. "Someone shoved these into my hand as I took you away from there."

I took them and pulled the package open. "God, I am a mess."

"You look amazingly beautiful." His smile, meant to lighten my heart, did the job — a little, at least.

I looked around the room at the things my mother used to use. "You've brought me into my mother's office."

"I did?" He looked around. "I just came in through the first door I could find to get you away from all that out there. This is the first room I found. Weird, huh?"

"I think it's a sign, to be honest. And I don't even believe in things like that." I blew my nose. "Or, at least, I used to not believe in things like signs and fate. Now, I'm not so sure what to believe."

Stone picked up a medical book off my mother's desk. "She was into medicine too?"

"She was a nurse." I strolled around the room my father had very rarely allowed me in. "Now, Dad didn't know this, but I had a spare key to this room that he used to keep locked up. Whenever I'd ask if I could come in here, he'd say he didn't like me messing with her things. So, after doing a lot of snooping around in his bedroom, I found a spare key in one of his drawers. I took that key and kept it locked away in my jewelry box. After that, I came in here often, sometimes two or three times a week. I would read the medical journals." I pointed them out on the bookshelf. "I've read every book that's in this room."

"So that's where your passion for medicine came from. See, you might not have gotten to know your mother in the flesh, but you definitely got to know her true spirit, and you even inherited it."

"Lily seems to have told you quite a lot in the short time you two had together." I felt a twinge of jealousy. "Seems I'll have to make this time I have with you count. We have to do some talking, Stone Nash, so we can get to know more about each other. So others won't have to keep filling us in."

"I agree." He pulled a book off the shelf. "To think that your mother's fingers moved along these pages, her hands held this book, that's amazing to me. And years later, you came to learn so much from her by reading these same books. Amazing how life works, isn't it?"

Looking at him as he thumbed through a book I'd read more times than I could count, I knew he was something special. "You came to me even when I told you not to. It takes a pretty committed man to do such a brave thing."

"I am *completely* committed to you," he nodded in agreement. "But I didn't screw off my dream to come to you, my love, so don't go on about that again. I've signed the lease at the hospital and put my engineer sister-in-law in charge of getting the bistro set up and ready for business. Another sister-in-law, Ember, is going to manage the place for me. She's already looking for suitable staff, and she'll make sure they have spotless backgrounds, too. I'm calling in help from everywhere on this."

"I could not be happier about that. I mean it." I knew he would pull it off.

"You don't even know the best part."

"What's the best part?" I asked as I sat in my mother's old desk chair, the wheels squeaking under my weight.

"The best part is that I've obtained a grant from my brothers and cousins, which I'll use to give one free meal a day to all the interns and residents at the hospital."

"They went for that?" I was genuinely surprised. "That's insane. But how long will that last?"

"For as long as it has to until the government grants can take its place. And I'll start this in your hospital and keep on going until all of Austin's hospitals are covered. Then I'll keep moving on from there. There will be a Healthy Hut Bistros in every hospital across America that will let me open one."

"Healthy Hut?" I had to laugh. "Really, Stone?"

"Yep." Shrugging his shoulders, he added, "The name just sort of grew on me. And after hearing everyone at your job saying, 'Welcome to Hamburger Hut, where the customers are number one and so are the burgers,' I knew I had to have a catchy greeting phrase too. Wanna hear it?"

I could not believe the man. "Let me hear it."

"Welcome to Healthy Hut, where your gut is number one and so is our food." He couldn't wipe the grin off his face.

"You're not going to make everyone say that every time someone walks in, are you?"

"Nah," he waved his hand as if waving away the silly notion. "But it will be written on a pin that everyone will have to wear on their shirts, right under their name tag. I've got another sister-in-law, Orla, coming up with uniforms. She and my brother Warner live in Ireland, but she can still do that from there. I'm learning just how small this world really is and how you can find help all over the place."

I glanced at the small mirror that hung on the wall across from the desk and found my eyes so puffy that it defied imagination. "Oh, God!" I slapped my hands over my eyes. "I need to get some ice on these. They're awful."

"You look fine," he said as he came to me, pulling me up into his arms then pressing his lips to mine. "You look like a woman who has just said her goodbyes to her father and mother. You look exactly the way you're supposed to."

"You're too sweet." I sucked in my breath as he moved his hand to rest against the valley of my lower back. "And too sexy."

"I can't believe all this. I can't believe how I feel about all this. It's sort of insane how great I feel about us right now. I mean, I love you, I do, but having a baby wasn't even on my radar. I figured you were on some kind of birth control. I didn't think this was even a possibility. But I'm feeling more and more — I guess you call it, giddy — with each moment that goes by. We're going to have a baby!"

Taking one of his hands, I placed it on my tummy. "So, let me get you up to speed. We are three weeks pregnant, and our baby is still in the embryo stage. It's about the size of a vanilla bean. I've been calling it my little vanilla bean. But in a short time, it will become a fetus, and I'm sure I'll give it another name by then."

He leaned down, moving his mouth close to my tummy.

"Hey there, little vanilla bean, this is your daddy. Be nice to your momma while you're in there, okay?"

I laughed and shook my head. "This is gonna take some getting used to."

*But I sure could get used to being with Stone, that is for sure.*

# CHAPTER 29
## STONE

I stood, looking around her mother's old office. "How did your parents meet, anyway? I mean, your dad was a wealthy man, and your mom was a nurse. I can't see them crossing paths."

"Dad was in a polo club. You know, where the men ride around on horses, which they call polo ponies because they're not as tall as most horses. Anyway, he fell off his and ended up in the hospital mom worked at. And they fell in love instantly."

"How long did they date before getting married?" I wanted to know lots more about the mother of my child.

"Not long. Six months after meeting, they got married. And nine months later, Lily was born. Three years after that, I came along." She dropped her head. "And ruined everything."

Taking her by the chin, I lifted her head to look at me. "The one thing I know is that God doesn't make any mistakes. My parents died when I was eight. There was a house fire, and they never made it out. For a long time, I felt like maybe I'd done something that caused that fire. You know, maybe I'd left on the stove or something like that. I didn't even use the stove back then, but there were all these questions in my mind. Baldwyn finally told me that no one was to blame for what had happened to them, even if one of us had made some mistake before we'd left for school that morning. God had this planned long before we were even born. So, I began to accept that as a fact. And I think you should too." I hated to see the pain she'd put herself in by taking on all the blame for her mother's death.

"I've been to many therapists over this. But you know what, you might be right. In my studies, I've learned the ins and outs of why some women die during childbirth. The body is fragile, and it doesn't take much to snuff the life out of it. And like you said, God must've had it planned for her all along." She nodded, wrapping her arms around me. "It's nice of you to care about me this way. Or should I just say that it's nice to feel cared for the way you make me feel?"

"There's gonna be plenty of caring coming from me from now on." Now that I knew there was a baby coming, I had to move things along a lot faster than I'd originally planned. "So, how about you tell me about who your father's right-hand man was?"

"William Langford and my father went to Yale together. They've been working together on this estate ever since my father inherited it. And to tell the truth, I would've been lost if it hadn't been for his guidance these past few days. I didn't know the first thing about setting up the funeral and finding life insurance policies. Mr. Langford walked me through everything, step by step."

"Then he is who you should hire to keep on doing what he's been doing with your father. That way, you can continue on your own journey to work on what you're passionate about." I expected to get some static from her on this.

"My passion has to take a back seat right now, Stone." She hugged me tightly, inhaling deeply. "Just knowing that you're going to be here for me whenever you can is enough."

"I'm here for you right now. And I'm here to tell you that there is no way in hell that your father wanted you to stop achieving your goals and pursuing your passion. That was never his intention. Had that heart attack not taken him well before his time, then he would've made sure things were properly set up to deal with this estate's business."

"I don't know, Stone. And what about Lily?"

"She's a grown woman. What about her?" I didn't think her older sister needed her as much as Jessa thought.

"She's a mess, Stone. I know you don't know her well at all, but she's such a drama queen. And she's as helpless as a little lamb. Plus, she's completely spoiled rotten and a total brat."

"Well, that's on her, isn't it?" I wasn't about to let her put a stop to her life for anyone. "You have a dream, and it's a good one. I think you've said the same words to me before. Your dream will help thousands or maybe even millions of people. That is the path you need to follow. *This* isn't *your* path, Jessa. And for the love of God, quit that job at Hamburger Hut already and use the money you have to pay for your schooling. And just so you know, you will not be moving back into that little apartment you've been living in. You're moving into my house." I held up one finger. "Let me say that the right way. You will move into *our* house, where *we* will raise *our* happy child *together*."

Her golden eyes sparkled as she looked at me. "I will?"

"You will. And you will continue with your plans — going to school, interning, and eventually, becoming a resident, and one day, a real doctor. Your parents would want that for you. And I'm not about to step out of your way so you can flush all that down the toilet. You were born to be a doctor, and by God, that's what you're gonna be."

"Come hell or high water?" she asked.

"Come hell or high water, baby." A kiss on her nose made her smile. "I like seeing that smile. Let's go out there so you can introduce me to your family and friends and that Mr. Langford guy who's gonna help you and your sister keep this thing going. Our kid's gonna be one wealthy little pipsqueak, that is for sure."

"But we will not spoil him or her. We will teach this kid that work is important and that they shouldn't merely live off the money others made for them." Her conviction clear on her face, she went on, "Promise me that, Stone."

"I promise that I won't spoil our kid. But I'll let you know this. I will love that kid with all my heart. So, if I do start to spoil it, open my eyes, and I'll stop."

"Deal." She took my hand, leading me out to meet the masses. "I'm gonna have some fun introducing you to everyone. What should I say you are to me?"

I laughed. "Tell them the truth. That I'm your baby-daddy."

Socking me in the shoulder, she huffed. "No way. You're my boyfriend. I don't want to tell anyone that we're expecting because it might jinx the pregnancy. So for now, this is our little secret."

"Aw, you're excited about having this baby, aren't you?" I hadn't pegged her for wanting a baby.

"It's grown on me. And yeah, I'm excited. And I'm happy that you're happy about it too. We're going to be alright. I think. I hope."

"We're going to be much better than just alright." We entered an enormous room full of people. I smelled some amazing smells, too. "There's food?"

"Lots and lots of food. It's how southerners deal with grief. People send all sorts of things to help the bereaved. A good thing for me, as I'm finally hungry, too."

We made our way through the crowd of people, with Jessa introducing me to the majority. I couldn't have recalled a name if I'd tried, so I just smiled and nodded, gave the usual nice to meet you too thing.

Then I heard her say, "This is my boyfriend, Mr. Langford. Allow me to introduce you to Stone Nash from Austin, Texas. He and his brothers own a resort there."

I gave him my biggest smile as I held out my hand. "It's

nice to meet you, Mr. Langford. Jessa's told me how important you were to her father and his family."

"Nice to meet you, too." He shook my hand. "Say, what's the name of your resort?"

"Whispers Resort and Spa."

"I've been there. I took my wife there about a year ago. That is some nice place you've got. State of the art, I might say." He looked pleased that it was my arm that Jessa was resting on. "Ray and I had been talking about something a while back."

"Ray's my dad's name," Jessa told me.

Nodding, I asked Mr. Langford, "What were you talking about?"

"Well, this estate is large. Much too large for just a couple of people to live in. There are so many empty bedrooms, you know. And the ballroom hasn't been used in years. We had the idea of turning this into either a resort or bed and breakfast. Many people seemed interested in staying at this historic home. And the staff could keep their jobs, too, so that would be nice. Miss Lily could stay right where she is staying now, in her suite of rooms. If that's what she wanted to do. Not much would change, except there would be more people around. But I think it would be good for this place."

Jessa looked at me with wide eyes. "That's some idea. What do you think?"

I wasn't sure what to think. "If you wanted, we could add it to our sister resorts. It could be called Whispers of North Carolina or something like that. That would make you and your sister our partners, if you wanted to do that. Of course, I would have to get our board's approval. But I think I could get that. There are a lot of perks if you join us, too. Tons of them, actually."

Jessa looked at her father's most trusted advisor. "That would take care of this place. But what about my father's business dealings? Who would handle them?"

"There's not much to handle. There's a law firm that handles the investments. They pay the taxes and deal with paying the employees as well. Your father had a check directly deposited into his account each quarter with the leftover revenue. You and your sister will need to give them your banking information so they can now split that between the two of you. Once a year, you should attend a meeting with them, just to keep yourselves abreast of what they're doing for you."

Jessa's jaw hung open. "Hang on. You are telling me that neither me nor Lily has to take over everything our father did to keep this place going and keep money making money?"

"He's been set up for years now. I mean, the man has kept himself busy with side investments in other companies. But you don't have to do that. Those were his pet projects. They don't have to become yours or your sister's."

Jessa still wasn't sure about things. "So, I don't have to quit medical school? And I can go back to Austin?"

"Of course, you can. Jessa, your father was extremely proud of you. He told everyone about how you were going to become a doctor. He would never leave you with so much to care for that it would get in the way of what you want."

She looked at me with tears in her eyes. "Stone, I'm coming home with you!" She looked back at Mr. Langford. "We're having a baby."

"Well, congratulations!"

*Looks like our little secret is out!*

# EPILOGUE

# JESSA

*One year later…*

Lily had come to Austin for our first board meeting since adding the estate to Whispers Resorts. She held our son, Liam, rocking him gently. "He's so handsome. I'm glad I finally got to come down to spend a week with you guys. But honestly, working at the resort back home has been a blessing to me. I love it. I love hobnobbing with all the guests, planning events, and my social status has gone through the roof. I tell you what?" She rubbed noses with the baby. "Little Liam, your Auntie Lily is having the time of her life."

"So no cousins for Liam in the near future?" I asked as we stepped off the elevator at the resort in Austin to sit in on the first meeting we'd been invited to.

"No way. I am not ready to settle down. Not at all." We walked into the room full of men, and my sister was in hog heaven. "Well, look at this. I've never seen so many handsome men in my life."

Stone came to us, kissing me then leaving a kiss on Lily's cheek. "Always the bell of the ball, aren't you?"

"Always." She handed the baby to Stone. "Here you go, Daddy. Your son has your gorgeous blue eyes, lucky devil."

Stone gave me a nod. "And his momma's blonde hair. Double lucky devil."

"Now, what are we gonna be talking about here at this meeting?" She took a seat, and I took one next to hers, and Stone sat next to me. "A round table," she pointed out. "Just like the knights of old had. Right?"

Baldwyn nodded. "We wanted to make a space for us to meet where there was no one person in charge. That way, you feel every bit as equal as the person sitting next to you."

"Very nice," Lily said as she looked around the table. "I feel special, sitting here with you all."

"We're excited to have you and Jessa joining us," Tyrell said. "Your resort has only been open for six months and has already made high profits. We couldn't be more pleased. And to hear that you're the one bringing in the clientele, Miss Lily — very impressive."

"I do try." She fanned herself. "Aw, it feels nice to be part of something."

Stone leaned over to whisper, "See, she came out of things just fine."

I was happy to see that Lily had found a passion too. "She sure did."

I hadn't had to do a thing with the estate — she'd worked with the advisors that Whispers Resort had sent over to turn the place into something out of a dream. Most of the time, my home felt like a nearly empty hotel. And now, it was a thriving resort, bringing joy to many.

Dad had left us something special, not the nightmare headache I'd thought we were inheriting. And I was able to remain faithful to my path, another year closer to becoming a doctor.

The meeting didn't last long. Afterward, Auntie Lily wanted to keep baby Liam in her room for the night so she could spend some quality time with him, since they didn't have plenty together. All I knew was that I was overjoyed to be spending some alone time with my guy.

Coming out of the bathroom, not wearing a single piece of fabric, I surprised Stone as he lay on the bed, channel surfing. He took one look at me and turned the television off, then tossed the remote on the floor as he began ripping his clothes off. "Oh, yeah!"

Once again, with the baby, time had gotten in the way of us having much of a sex life. So, I was not going to let this night go by without pleasing my man. "I hope you've consumed lots of liquids to help you through this sexual journey I'm about to take you on, babe."

He picked up the bottle of water off the nightstand, gulping it down. "I'm ready."

Laughing, I flew into his open arms then wrapped my legs around his waist. "This is one of my most favorite places to be in. Right in your arms."

"I love you being in them too." He kissed me hard, as it took us no time at all to find that passion we shared. He carried me to the bed, laying me down as he moved his body over mine, pressing himself into me, connecting us in such a way that made my heart pound only from our connection.

Life couldn't have been any sweeter than it was, living with him and our son. Stone was an amazing man who'd gotten his bistro up and going, with lines running along the hospital's hallways as people waited to get to taste one of Chef Nash's many creations.

Stone had gotten used to being called Chef Nash, and even showed a fair amount of pride that people had started calling him that. I was proud to be a huge part of his life. But I wanted just a little bit more.

I wasn't sure if he was on the same page that I was, though. So after we made love and lay in a pile of messed up sheets and blankets, I dug deep to find the courage to ask him something that had been building inside of me since our son's birth. He'd stayed right there with me throughout everything that had to do with our pregnancy. He was the man I was meant to spend my life with, and now I knew that without a shadow of a doubt.

My arm draped over his body, I kissed his chest before looking up at him. "Stone, do you ever think about getting married?"

"To who?" he teased me.

I smacked him in the chest. "Me, you fool."

"Is that a proposal?" he asked.

"If it is, what would you say to it?" I bit my lip, not completely sure he was into the idea just yet.

"If you're asking me to marry you, then I'm saying hell yes." He reached over, taking something out of the nightstand, then held up a little black box. "It seems like I've been thinking the same thing as you. I picked this up this morning."

He opened the box, revealing an insane engagement ring. "Oh, my God!" I held out my hand, wiggling my fingers. "Put it on me!"

As he slid that ring onto my finger, I felt my heart burst wide open. "I love you so much."

"I love you too, baby. And soon we'll be man and wife and continue this happy life."

*A dream come true.*

# STONE

*Six months later...*

Our wedding was held at the North Caroline resort, the estate that had once been Jessa's home. We'd invited everyone we knew to come and stay. I stood at the end of the aisle in the ballroom as Jessa made her way towards me.

A long, flowing white gown with a long train glided across the dark wood floor with such elegance it made me want to cry. But as soon as I looked at her gorgeous face, I could only smile.

She handed her bouquet of flowers to her sister, her maid of honor, then took my hands into hers. "You look amazing," I told her.

"You're the most handsome man in this room." She looked around at all the people there. "And that's saying something."

"Aww." She knew how to make me blush sometimes.

Lily leaned in. "What about me? How do I look?"

Jessa gave her a look that asked her to step back. "Come on, this is my day, remember?"

"Sorry." She leaned back. "Go on."

We repeated all the words the preacher told us to say, and I meant every word of it. When he said that I could kiss my bride, I kissed the hell of her before we turned to face a cheering crowd. "Woo! Hoo!" I shouted.

Yee-haws and more southern hoots and hollers were made right back to me. All the while, my wife's smile wouldn't leave her face. It was the second-best day of my life. Liam's birth had to have the number one spot. A baby is a real miracle. I'd witnessed that myself.

After our dancing was done and my wife and I were allowed to leave the dancefloor, I spotted some of our cousins from down in the valley of Texas hanging out at the open bar.

"So, how are the Duran brothers doing this fine evening?" I asked as I bellied up to the bar. "I need a beer, stat." I liked using medical terminology, even if I wasn't sure what stat was short for.

Cayce, the oldest of the four brothers, answered, "We're damn good, cousin. Thanks for inviting us to your wedding."

Chase was second in line. "We needed to get the hell out of Dodge for a while. And by Dodge, I mean Brownsville. We've been using all our scientific engineering brains for this man, but he won't even listen to our ideas. It's grown bothersome."

"You guys are all working together?" I hadn't known that.

Callan, the third one in line, answered, "Yeah. But I've got to tell you that our boss not listening to our ideas is making us rethink the industry we're in. I mean, I know we're supposed to be thinking about things that have to do with weaponry, but how many weapons does he expect us to come up with?"

The baby of their family, Chance, spoke up. "Sorry for my brothers. They're just tired of our boss. This is a great wedding, man. I can't believe what you guys have done for yourselves. It's amazing."

"Thanks." I took a long drink of the cold beer. "So, what kinds of ideas do y'all have anyway?" I was curious, as these guys were all highly educated. When they were younger, their parents had split up, and neither had wanted to keep them, so they were put into a children's home. It was a sad story, but they did end up being able to go to college for free, so their unhappy childhood paid off in that way. But what a price to pay.

Cayce lit up like a torch. "Okay, so we've come up with this idea of making something that can convert ocean waves into electricity. We live near South Padre on the Gulf of Mexico, so we've been able to try out small projects, and we've actually managed to get small amounts of electricity. But we need more supplies, and we thought, very incorrectly, that our filthy rich boss would want in on this."

"But he didn't," I said, nodding as some ideas began bouncing around in my head. "If you guys have a valid plan and could come and make a nice presentation, I can set up a meeting with my brothers and the Gentry brothers. We're all in this to help our family make the most out of themselves. How long do you think it would take you guys to get that together?"

Chase scratched his head, pushing back his black cowboy hat as he did. "You know what? I think we could put that all together by next month. Think you could get us a meeting sometime in May?"

"You got it. It's all about family with us. You guys will see. And, for the record, I think making electricity out of ocean waves is a badass idea. Now, the only thing you have to do to join our elite group is come up with a name for your company that includes the word Whisper. Think you can do that?"

Cayce was quick to say, "Whispering Waves Technology."

My brows rose, as I thought he'd hit the nail right on the head. "You might just have something there, boys. Only time will tell. See you in May."

*And our happily ever afters just keep on coming.*

**The End.**

9 781639 700387